...AND NOW MIGUEL

...AND NOW MIGUEL

Joseph Krumgold

Illustrated by Jean Charlot

SCHOLASTIC INC.
New York Toronto London Auckland Sydney

ISBN 0-590-43297-4

12 11   4 5 6 7 8 9/0

Printed in the U.S.A.   40

First Scholastic printing, January 1990

For
my son
ADAM

...AND NOW MIGUEL

CHAPTER 1

I AM Miguel. For most people it does not make so much difference that I am Miguel. But for me, often, it is a very great trouble.

It would be different if I were Pedro. He is my younger brother, only seven years old. For Pedro everything is simple. Almost all the things that Pedro wants, he has—without much worry.

I wanted to find out how it was with him one day when we were in our private place near the Rio Pueblo, the river that goes through our farm. I asked him "Pedro, suppose you could have anything you want. Is there anything you want?"

"Ai, of course." He looked up from reaching below a rock in the river. In this way we catch trout, slowly feeling around in the quiet places beneath big stones. If the fish comes by, sliding soft against your hand, you can catch him. Pedro was just learning to fish like this. He looked up, not wishing to talk. "Of course, sure I want something."

"Like what?"

"Like not so much school."

"School—yes. But that is something that you do *not* want."

"Like I say—not so much."

"Then what is it that you *do* want?"

"Shh!" He closed his eyes, moving his hand slowly, slowly in the water, holding his breath, with his tongue between his teeth.

Of a sudden he grabbed, splashing. He made a big commotion in the water. It was no good. Even before he took his hand out of the water, I knew it was empty.

"A good big trout, that's what I do want." Pedro looked at me like he was mad at me, like I spoiled his chance for the fish. "A good one, six inches big!"

He was mad. He took a stone and threw it into the water with all his might.

So I caught him a trout. It is not so hard. You lay down with your hand in the water, in a place where there are shadows below the bank. You leave your hand there for a long time, until the fish see that it is nothing strange. Until

2

they come by, even touching you. Until you can touch them, even rub them very lightly. They seem to like this, the fish, for you to rub them this way. Then when you feel them coming through your fingers, slowly you hold on to them, slowly but tight. Without any sudden move. And that's that.

I gave the fish to Pedro. It was almost six inches. He was happy with me again.

That's the way it is with Pedro. One such fish, not too big after all, and he is happy.

It is enough for him for everything to be like it is.

When the sun shines hot and dry and he can go swimming in the pool where the river goes around the farm of my Uncle Eli, that for Pedro is enough.

And when it rains, that too is enough. He is a great artist, Pedro. He sits in the kitchen when there is thunder outside, and all the pictures in his book he turns yellow and red and blue with his crayons.

If there is a ball, he will play ball. And if there is not, he will roll an old tire. No matter which, he is content.

It would be good to be Pedro. But how long can you stay seven years old? The trouble with me is that I am Miguel.

It would be good to be Gabriel. He is also my brother, and he is nineteen years old. Next to my Grandfather, and my Uncle Bonifacio, and my Uncle Eli, and next to my father who is called Old Blas, and my biggest brother who is called Young Blas and who wears a badge and drives the school bus, Gabriel is the greatest man in the world.

Everything that Gabriel wants, he can get. He explained this to me one Friday last winter.

All week long Gabriel goes to the high school in Taos, which is a very big town eight miles away, of one thousand people and many stores that sell marshmallow candy. This year Gabriel will graduate from high school. And that will be too bad for the basketball team and the baseball team as well as for the Future Farmers of America, a club of which he is president. From Monday to Friday Gabriel goes to school and wins the games there and is a president. But on Friday he forgets all these things and helps my uncles and my father with the sheep.

In our family there is always one thing, and that is the

sheep. The summer passes and the winter comes and soon it is Easter and the time for spring; but all the time, no matter when, there is the sheep. In our house we may be very happy. Like the time my littlest sister, Faustina, was born. Or very sad. Like when Young Blas was hurt by the mowing machine. But these things they come and go. Everything comes and goes. Except one thing. The sheep.

For that is the work of our family, to raise sheep. In our country, wherever you find a man from the Chavez family, with him will be a flock of sheep. It has been this way for many years, even hundreds, my grandfather told me. Long before the Americans came to New Mexico, long before there was any such thing here called the United States, there was a Chavez family in this place with sheep. It was even so in Spain where our family began. It is even so today.

And so when Gabriel finishes school for the week, on Friday, he goes out to the sheep camp. There he takes the place of one of my uncles or my father, and the older man can come home for a day or two.

In the winter we pasture our sheep on the big mesa that stretches from the cliffs on the other side of our river, far, far north, flat and straight almost into Colorado. This wide plain spreads out to the west to the Rio Grande river where there is a deep arroyo, a great canyon that goes down, down into the earth to where the big river flows. The land is owned by the Indians of the Taos Pueblo and my father pays the war chief of these Indians ten cents every month for each

5

sheep that we pasture. We are very good friends with the Indians. It was not always so, my father tells me, but now we are good friends.

The sheep camp is built into a wagon, so that it can be moved as the sheep are driven from where they have eaten to new pasture. It has a bed built in, and shelves, and a stove. No matter how hard it snows or how cold it gets, inside the sheep wagon it is always tight against the wind and dry and warm.

On this Friday the wagon was in a place very near to the Rio Grande canyon, almost twelve miles from our house. Gabriel went there with the pick-up truck, and he took me along. Driving the truck is very hard. There are no roads. You drive right across the mesa through the mesquite bushes, keeping away from the big holes and the big rocks. It is wise to drive slow and be careful.

But Gabriel did not drive slow, yet he was still careful. He swung the big truck from side to side like it was a little stick, and all the time he sang a beautiful song about a red flower.

"Miguel," he turned to me after he had finished with the song, "what's up with you? You haven't opened your mouth since we left the house."

"Me?" I stopped looking at the bushes and the rocks. "As for me, I've been thinking."

"About what?"

"About how easy it is for you—." Gabriel swung the

wheel, and the truck skidded in the snow away from a big hole. "Well, how easy it is for you—to be Gabriel."

Gabriel laughed. "Easier for me than anyone else in the world. After all, that's who I am."

"But it is not so easy for me—to be Miguel."

"Maybe not." Gabriel smiled, watching the snow ahead. "It takes a little time. Wait a year or two, and it'll be easier."

"Only to wait? Isn't there something else I can do? Like —practice?"

"Being Miguel—it's not like playing basketball. No, it's a hard thing to train for."

The truck was going faster. Gabriel was looking through the windshield, his eyes a little closed and tight, like he was looking into the wind. But now that we were talking about such important things, there was much that I wanted to know.

"There must be a secret! Some kind of a special secret, isn't there?"

"For what?" It was hard to talk now, the truck was roaring so much because we were going so fast.

"How to get to be a president." I had to yell. "So easy. And when you want a deer, you take a horse and in a day or two you come back with a deer. And the house?"

"What house?" Gabriel yelled back at me.

"The house by the cottonwood tree. You're going to build such a house of adobe?"

"Sure. Someday."

"And you're going to become an engineer? At the college?"

"Uh-huh."

"How?" I had to shout real loud. "How is all this done—so easy—to get what you wish?" I took him by the arm because he didn't seem to be hearing. "How?"

"Mike!" He shoved me away, back into the corner of the seat. "Lay off. Coyote."

I looked off to one side where Gabriel nodded with his head. And there it was, racing away for the edge of the mesa, no bigger than a dog, than our sheep dog Cyclone. He was just a speck, the coyote, moving against the snow. They are terrible animals for the sheep. Every year they kill many lambs, sometimes more than two dozen. They are smart and they are faster than a bird.

But with Gabriel driving we were getting closer. There was no more time to be careful. Into holes and over rocks we went, and I held on or else I would hit the ceiling of the truck with my head. We pulled closer. I could watch the coyote, moving like a fist that opens and closes quicker than you can blink your eyes. A shadow sliding across the snow.

"Reach down," Gabriel spoke quick. "In back of the seat."

I got the rifle that was there and held it. At just the right moment, Gabriel stamped on the brakes. Before the car even stopped skidding in the snow, Gabriel had pulled off one of his gloves, grabbed the gun and was sighting it. I hardly knew he'd taken it out of my hands before I heard it crack.

The coyote stopped in the middle of a leap. As if a tight

wire was stretched in his path and caught him. But when he dropped he continued on his way, not so fast but he still kept going.

Gabriel took his time, carefully holding the animal in the sights of the rifle. He actually hummed the song about the red flower as he took his time. He tightened his finger on the trigger.

The second bullet stopped the coyote for good. And Gabriel laughed. It was good to kill a coyote. With two bullets, many lambs were saved. Gabriel laughed because it was good and because it was so easy.

That's the way it was with Gabriel. Everything that he wants he can get. With Pedro, it is the opposite. Everything that he has is enough.

Both of them, they are happy.

But to be in between, not so little anymore and not yet nineteen years, to be me, Miguel, and to have a great wish—that is hard.

I had such a wish. It was a secret and yet not a secret. For how secret can you keep high mountains that one can see for hundreds of miles around, mountains that face me when I first open my eyes every morning and are the last thing I see in the night.

This was my wish, to go up there—into those mountains that are called the Mountains of the Sangre de Cristo.

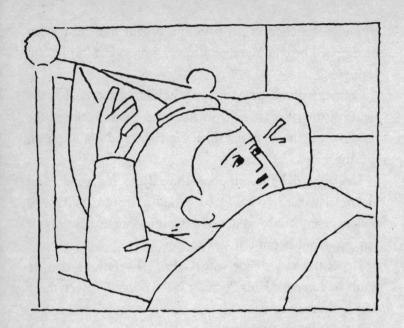

CHAPTER 2

THERE is one thing to say right away about the Sangre de Cristo Mountains and it is this. They are wonderful.

I don't know if it is true but I have been told that if you are good all the time and if sometimes you pray, then you will go to heaven. Maybe this is so and maybe not.

But about the Sangre de Cristo Mountains I know for sure. If you are ready and the time comes, then that's all. You will go.

To get to be ready, it is first necessary to be of my family, a Chavez, and that I have come to be without even trying.

10

Then, one must be a shepherd and know all about how to take care of the sheep. It is likewise a help to know how to bake bread and be a good cook as well as to ride a horse and shoot a gun and catch fish. When you can do these things then you are ready.

And all that must be done then is to wait until the time comes.

And it always does. Every year. It comes as sure as the time for the lambs to be born, and the time for the Fiesta de San Ysidro, and then the shearers arrive and the wool is clipped. Just so sure as all these things happen, comes the time for the flock to go up into the Mountains of the Sangre de Cristo.

Then you will go along. If, that is, everyone knows you are ready.

But if they don't, then you must wait again for another whole year. And even another year and another.

Each year, after the last heavy snows are over, the time comes to show that I am ready and that it is different this year for me, Miguel, than it was last year. It is in this early part of the year that the new lambs are born. Then the sheep are brought in from the pueblo land of the Indians, from the big mesa where they have spent the winter. The sheep wagon is brought in too. Now the flock must stay close to the house so that everyone can help with the birth of the lambs.

At this time there is no question of who is Pedro and who is Gabriel and who am I. Everyone helps without it making any difference who he is.

11

Even in the middle of the night someone can come into the bedroom where Faustina sleeps in one bed and me and Pedro in another. This one can say, "Come on, they need water."

There is no question who asks for the water or who goes to fetch it. We are quick to find our clothes and run to the spring, which is down the hill behind the tool shed. We carry the water to where it is needed, to the lambing pens where the fires are kept going all night and the men must help the newest lambs who are having a hard time to get born. Or to the kitchen where my mother is always cooking, during this time, because someone is always eating.

The lambs come at all different hours, and all our uncles and cousins stay at our house to be ready to help, and there is no breakfast time or dinner time or bed time. Everyone sleeps and eats when he can, no matter who he is, as long as he is ready when something is needed.

I would like it to matter who he is, especially if it's me, Miguel. But that has never happened.

"Behind the tractor," my father will talk to me without even turning around, "in the tool shed there on the shelf is the liniment. The brown bottle. Hurry!"

My father will be busy bending over a ewe who tries hard to give birth to a lamb, working together with Uncle Eli. He will not even look up when I bring the medicine and put it into his hand.

Once I tried to make my father see who I am. When he asked for some burlap bags to wrap one small lamb who was cold, I brought him the bags. When he took them from me, I said, "Here are the bags."

My father said nothing. He rubbed the lamb and wrapped it up.

"All right?" I said. "Okay?"

My father felt the neck of the lamb. "He'll be all right. It'll live."

"No," I shook my head. "I ask about the bags."

"What about the bags?"

"Are they all right?"

"What can be wrong with bags?"

"Wrong? Nothing. Except sometimes—." This was not what I wanted to talk about at all. "There can be holes in them."

"For our purpose, to wrap up new lambs, holes make no difference. That's why we use old bags."

I knew all this. But I couldn't stop him from saying it.

"If we wanted to put something into them, like grain or wool, then we use new bags without holes." My father stood up now, looking down at me. "You didn't bring me any of the new wool bags, those that are in the corner of the shearing shed?"

"Me?" I said quickly. "Not me!" This is why it is hard for me to be Miguel sometimes, getting people to understand.

"Then what is all this talk about bags?" My father put his hands in the back pockets of his pants and waited.

"I'm sorry." I looked around trying to find some way to leave. But it was too late.

13

"Miguel, what's the trouble?"

"Nothing." When my father looks at you then there is no place to go. "It's only that I wanted you to know that it was me—I brought you the bags when you asked for them."

"Of course. They were needed. That's why I asked."

"I know, but—" It was no use. It could not get any better. "That's all."

"Ai Blas." Uncle Bonifacio yelled to my father from across the corral. "This ewe here, with twins. Look's bad."

"Be right with you," my father called to him, but he looked back. "Let me understand this, Miguel. This is nothing but a question of bags, yes?"

"That's all."

"Nothing else?"

"No."

"Very well," said my father, and he hurried through the sheep to the other side of the corral.

It is different in school. There when the teacher asks you to write in your book the capital of the State of New Mexico, and you write "Sante Fe," the matter does not come to an end. If you do what she asks, then you get a star in your book. And after you get enough stars you get a G on your report card instead of an F.

To be sure it is always good to have a card with a G instead of an F. Though, to tell the real truth, I never found it made so much difference from one day to the next what kind of letter you had on the card.

But here with the family and with the sheep, where it makes a big difference, to bring an old bag is nothing but the question of a bag. And if you talk about it, all you do is to get into trouble. And liniment is nothing else but liniment. And when you bring water that is the end of it. There are no stars.

And here, too, it makes a big difference from one day to the next. For soon the days pass and all the lambs are born, and then the shearers arrive and not many days are left.

And even though everyone gets busy again at the shearing, it's not like when the lambs come. To shear and to bag the wool, to tie the fleeces, you have to be an expert to do these things. Even a little mistake is bad. All I can do is to sit on a fence, with Pedro, and watch the others hard at work under the shearing sheds.

"And after so many years," like I once told Pedro, "it's not enough, just to watch anymore."

"Why?" said Pedro. "This is fine. Nothing to do. No school. What could be better than this?"

"It would be better to help, like our brother Blas over there, pushing the sheep into the pen for the shearers."

"Such hard work. What for?"

I had not told Pedro, or anyone else, about my wish to go to the Sangre de Cristo. Nor did I tell him now. Instead I said, "When we work with the others, as at the lambing, we are less by ourselves. It is not so lonesome."

"We're together," said Pedro. "That's not lonesome."

"I mean alone by ourselves. When the others are working."

"You know as good as I do," said Pedro, "when we run and fetch and help at lambing time, no one even knows we're there."

This is true, as I have said. "But even so, it would be better to help," I said once again. "Much better."

"It is better to be sitting here on the fence," said Pedro, "just watching and doing nothing else."

That's the way it is with Pedro. Everything he has is enough. But for me, I have the wish to be part of everything that happens, even if it is not happening to me. Like when the shearers leave and the day comes for the men to leave with the flock, to start for the Mountains. Even though I have never gone with the others, that day for me is a bigger day than Christmas.

Hardly anyone goes to sleep because the start is very early in the morning, before it gets light, and because there is so much to prepare. We all work to get everything together the men will need—the horses and a tent, the blankets and the food and the guns and a stove. Each man who is going must take everything for the whole time he is away.

And I, too, in secret, have for many years now prepared a bundle for myself which I keep underneath the bed without anyone knowing. In it I put all my clothes of the winter though it is by then summer, because it is cold, they have told me, on the high ridges and on the top peaks. In it, too, I pack my best fish hooks, the luckiest ones. I put this bundle

16

beneath my bed because you never know. It could happen at the very last that my father, or my brother Blas, or Uncle Eli will say, "One moment, Miguel. It has been decided among us that you are ready and that this year you will come with the flock, with the rest of us, to the Sangre de Cristo. You are needed."

"If I am needed," I will say, "then of course I will be glad to go."

Then they will say, "The only trouble is we forgot to tell you until it is late. Can you get ready in time?"

And because my bundle is already under the bed, I will say, "Yes. Sure. No trouble."

It could happen this way. Though it never has. But until the very last minute, until the very start, the chance remains that it might. And until then it is good to be in our house. For everyone talks of nothing but the Mountains of the Sangre de Cristo. And because the men are going away for so long, not less than three months, they like to talk to the rest of us who are staying. Even when Faustina cries because they are leaving my father will stop his work and take her on his lap.

"Tinga mia," he will tell her. "It is not forever. At the end of the summer we will be back."

"Why?" Faustina squeaks very high like a lamb when she cries. "Why don't you stay here, in the house?"

"We must feed the sheep. There is good grass, the best in the world, on the the Sangre de Cristo."

"Here is grass. On the farm is grass. What's grass?"

18

My father always has to wipe her nose. It runs like a spring when she cries. "There's not enough, Tinga," he tells her. "For so many sheep. On this farm we can feed no more than fifty sheep. We have many hundreds and each one with a lamb. That's why in the winter we must rent from the Indians to pasture the flock. You remember how it is in the winter?"

"Yes," says Faustina. If my father holds her long enough on his lap pretty soon she quiets down.

"But in the summer the pueblo lands on the mesa get very dry. There is very little grass for the sheep to eat. We are lucky we have the mountains so close. Up there it is never dry. The grass is always green and rich. It makes the sheep and the lambs fat and healthy. Isn't that good, Tinga?"

"Okay," says Faustina, as if she understood what it was all about.

The truth is we are lucky indeed to be able to take the sheep to the Sangre de Cristo. Not everyone can go there for pasture. All this was explained to me by Uncle Bonifacio.

"No one owns the mountains." We were packing flour and bacon and all kinds of food in bags when he told me this. "No one except the government. And the government name for the Sangre de Cristo is the Carson National Forest."

"Carson—he is part of the government."

"No, he's just a man by the name Kit Carson who fought with the Indians and killed buffaloes and was a soldier, and now he is dead. So instead of putting up a statue for him where the birds can sit when they get tired of sitting in trees, they set aside the mountains so that no one can own them and gave his name, Carson, to the whole place." Uncle Bonifacio smiled as we kept putting food into the bags. Often he smiles, my Uncle Bonifacio, but I have never seen him laugh.

"Now people come from far away to go up in the mountains because it is beautiful there."

"Like I say," I said. "Wonderful."

"That's also true." Uncle Bonifacio nodded. "Wonderful. Almost anything you like, you can find in the mountains. Great sights to see. Good fishing, bass in the lakes and trout everywhere. Animals to hunt, in the proper season, even bears and wolf and deer."

"And lions and tigers?"

"There are mountain lions. But tigers? This is the Sangre de Cristo after all, Miguel, not a traveling circus. And there are trees everywhere, good for making lumber if one gets permission from the government and promises not to cut down all the trees. In which case the birds would have to go back to the statues after all. And fine pasture for cattle and sheep. But in order to graze your stock on the mountains you must also get permission, and this is difficult."

"With the mountains so big? Stretching as far as you can see?"

"Even so, there are men in the government who say even less sheep should graze in the Sangre de Cristo than now. For there is a danger if all the grass is eaten. Then when it rains on the bare earth the dirt will wash away, and the water will run off the hills as from a roof, making one day a flood and the next day dry, bare rocks under the sun. That is why only a few are given the permit to pasture their sheep in the mountains. And that is why we of the Chavez family are lucky to have such a permit."

"Thank goodness we are lucky!"

"Thank goodness if you wish," Uncle Bonifacio closed the bag now and tied it up, "but also thank your grandfather for being such a wise man. It was he, many years ago, who got the permit for our flock. If not for him you would have to be a policeman when you grow up, or an airplane pilot," he smiled.

I don't think to be a policeman or an airplane pilot is anything so terrible. But still I am glad that I am growing up to be a shepherd, if only it doesn't take too long. And so, as Uncle Bonifacio said, I thanked my grandfather.

It was during the last hour of the night. I helped my grandfather tie the canvas bag filled with blankets onto the mule, Herman. My grandfather is almost eighty years, which is as old as most people get. He no longer goes to the mountains but nothing is done without his help. Tying the pack, he worked very slow and every knot was tight. He stopped and shook his head when I thanked him.

"The permit, it is only a piece of paper of the government. The paper will go and the government will go, but still the mountains will remain where the good Lord put them. It is He you should thank."

"Yes, Padre de Chavez," I said. "I will, next Sunday when we go to Mass."

"Be sure to thank him for everything," he said. He turned from the mule and slowly he pointed with his hand from the north to the south. It was not yet dawn, but already the sky looked to be in two parts. The part that was really the sky was not so dark, and the part that was the mountains still black. "When you wish to see what is ahead, in the time to come, you look to the mountains. If it is white on their peaks with snow, like blessed white clouds that have come to rest, it will be a good year. There will be much water all through the months from the snows that melt, and we and the sheep will have it good, here and far from here. All down the Rio Grande valley, they will rejoice. Even in Texas and Arizona and in Old Mexico they will give thanks to the Lord that he has placed here the Mountains of the Sangre de Cristo. Give thanks, too, Miguel, for the year that is ahead."

"Next Sunday," I promised. "For sure."

And I did. Though last year, when we spoke, it was not the year for which I wanted to thank anybody. Last year it happened like all the years before.

When the time came, my father kissed my mother and then each one of us. Then we all went outside, and everybody hugged everybody else and said goodbye. No one said anything special to me, not even at the last moment.

One could see the mountains with the tops all white as they started out, for it was getting day. Gabriel was on his horse Blackie, leading the three pack horses. And Uncle Eli,

too, was on a horse. My father, my brother Blas, and Uncle Bonifacio went on foot, driving the flock with the dog Cyclone.

We stood watching them. My mother stood with my grandfather, and my big sisters were with the little ones, Faustina and Pedro. And me, not big or little, I stood there alongside the others.

The flock sent up a big cloud of dust as it started out. And after awhile there was nothing to watch but this brown, dirty cloud coming up and moving slowly toward the high mountains. By then the others had gone back into the house. Soon, even the dust of the cloud disappeared, and nothing was left to look at except the tops of all the Mountains of the Sangre de Cristo, standing clean and shining and high in the sun. At the end it was no good to stand there any more looking up at them. It made you to feel more little than you are.

So I went back into the house. I took the bundle out from underneath the bed. I put everything back in its place.

It happened this way last year. And that is the last time, I have promised myself, it will happen in such a way. For now it is a new year, with the winter coming to an end, and I have become twelve.

CHAPTER 3

"I AM here! Here. The time has come and I am here! I am here!"

The last thing I heard was the clock in the kitchen going nine, ten, eleven times. So now it must be midnight or maybe even after. That's when I heard it. The cry of the first lamb of the New Year. I heard it coming in through the window of the bedroom, from far away off on the prairie, a little sound all alone in the wide night that was bright with the moon.

"Look what's happened," the lamb cried. "Me."

25

It didn't speak the words, of course. It didn't even sound like the words. The cry of the lamb sounded like my friend Juby, at school, when he tries to yell far away and at the same time he keeps coughing. Not like words. But it stands to reason. What else could a new lamb, especially the first lamb born in the whole flock, once he got to his feet and opened his mouth to baa—what else would he say?

"Me! I'm here."

Without taking my head from the pillow, I listened until I was sure. Then I folded back the comforter, and slipped my feet out from Pedro's legs, and took away his arm from around my neck. One would think that Pedro, who sleeps with me in the same bed, was training to be a wrestling champion, the way he sleeps.

Without opening his eyes, Pedro said, "Right away," for this is how he wakes up every morning. When he says "right away" it means that right away he'll get up and have breakfast and go to school.

But he never does. And even though no one believes him any longer, he still says "right away" when he wakes up, as if it were his morning prayers. The truth is, to get Pedro out of bed it is necessary to pull him by the feet, and let him fall on the floor, and then bend the mattress in half so there's no more bed anymore he can get back into.

Faustina. who sleeps on the other side of our bedroom, she heard me too.

"Miguel?"

26

"Yes."

"I'm thirsty."

"Down here there is no water." I was underneath the bed looking for my shoes.

"Where d'you think you're going?" Pedro looked down at me from over the side of the bed. He was actually awake.

"It's started. The lambing. I just heard it—the first lamb. I'm going to go and have a look."

"Yah!" Faustina hiccuped and giggled. "He's gonna go look."

"That's what you think," said Pedro.

"Now's bedtime." The way Faustina laughed 'way high up, you'd think this was one big joke.

"In order to grow, we gotta stay in bed," said Pedro. "You know that."

"For you, yes." I didn't even wait to get dressed. I started out with my arms filled with clothes. "I've had enough growing."

I was the first one out of the house, where only my mother and big sisters slept these nights. The men stayed with the flock out in the fields and in the corrals, sleeping in the sheep wagon and around camp fires, waiting for many nights now for the lambs to start. And now, surely, it had begun. Out on the veranda where I finished to dress myself, I heard it even more clearly.

"Baa. Aah. It's me. I'm here."

"Mickey. What are you doing?" It was my sister Tomasita.

She was all wrapped around with a bathrobe. "It's not allowed. Go back."

"I know." I was trying to put one leg in my pants, while balancing, and without looking. "I know—but that was last year. Now could be different."

"No, Miquito. Go back!" Tomasita hurried down the path, through the wooden gate to the corrals. And the screen door behind me banged again. I couldn't see who it was because my head was all caught in my jersey, because I was trying to get dressed so fast.

"You'd better watch out, Mike, Mother's coming." It was Leocadia, who is next to my biggest sister.

"Maybe she'll let me."

"Maybe." Leocadia helped me to push my head through the hole in the top of the jersey. "But I don't think so. She'll say you must wait."

"A whole year more?"

"Until morning." Leocadia pulled the jersey down in the back. "You can see the new lamb in the morning." And she was off after Tomasita.

It was not a question of morning, to wait until morning. But to be with the others from the very start this time. That might make all the difference.

I was putting on the second shoe when my mother came out.

"Miguelito!" My mother was surprised to see me, yet she spoke softly for no one to hear, even though there was no one around who could listen. Only Cyclone, the dog, who was tied to the fence. He started to bark.

"If you will let me tell you something, there is something I have to tell you," I told her. "Like the way I worked hard all the winter. And at school. There was no day in which there was not a new star in my book. You yourself said no one worked harder at the ditching."

This had happened only the week before, the ditching. That is the time at the end of the winter when all the families who live along the same irrigation ditch come together to clean up the ditch. This is in order to make everything ready for when the fields are plowed and the seed is planted. Then to get water coming down the ditch and onto the fields, it is best to have all the rocks and bushes and mud from the winter out of the ditch.

There are many families on our ditch, more than a dozen, stretching from where we live to our village of Los Cordovas. But concerning the ditch, everyone listens to Mr. Martinez, who is of my mother's family, for he is the *Mayor Domo* of the ditch. In English this means he is the ditch boss, and among us a new one is elected every year to tell each family what to do, and how many days of water each can have, and what days he can let the water into his own fields.

At ditching time each family is supposed to bring so many men to work for so many days. And my father let me stay home from school in order that I, too, could go along to help. Mr. Martinez said I could count for a half a man,

29

which is not too great a thing, and I asked my father to speak with Mr. Martinez in order that I should be counted three quarters of a man at least. But when he did so, everyone laughed, including my father, because at ditching time everyone does laugh most of the time, and there is a lot of singing as well as wine and other things to drink.

The question though was settled fine. It was agreed that even though I would remain one half a man, since the next day was Saturday and I didn't have to go to school, I would be allowed to work two full days. So that I did end up being counted as one whole man. This was perfect for me, and better for everyone since fractions are hard to keep straight anyway.

To prove it was no mistake I worked as good as I could, using only the biggest shovels and the biggest pickaxes. So that my mother that night made me eat a third mutton chop, just like the older men, because I had worked so hard. And I ate it, too, easily.

And now, when I reminded her, she remembered it all.

"I know," she said. "You already have become one whole man, Miguel. But even a whole man must learn to wait until his time comes. He can work, and he can prepare, but he must know how to wait, too."

"I've learned how to wait. In twelve years, I've learned."

"Is it so hard, then, to wait until morning?"

"Another year. That's how long it will be. This time comes just once every year."

"Miguel!" My mother stopped me. She held me by the

chin, tight. She wiped her apron at my eyes. "I have watched you using all your strength to open the gate to the barnyard, the one from which the big stone hangs. But this is not like a gate. To become something different from what you are, it takes more than being strong. Even a little time is needed as well. No, no!" She wouldn't let me speak. "Go back with the others, with Faustina and Pedro."

"They will be glad to see me!" I kicked off one of my shoes. Not hard. Just enough to hit the door a good bang.

"Back to bed or we'll see about this!" When my mother says, we'll see about this, sometimes it can hurt. I picked up my shoe and started into the house. When I looked back she was untying Cyclone, who was barking, so that even he could go.

Everybody, even the dog, got out that night to see the first lamb.

"And you," said Pedro. He was waiting for me with a smile on his face. "Did you get a good look?"

I didn't answer. With my shoe, I took aim at the floor and let it go. First one, then the other. What difference how much noise I made?

"Okay!" yelled Faustina. "Okay. Okeydokee!" Every few days Faustina learns a new word, and then that's the only word she uses. It doesn't mean anything.

"It's sure nice when someone grows enough." Pedro kept talking behind my back. I sat on the edge of the bed, pulling off my clothes, and he kept talking and laughing. "Everything's sure nice. They get up in the middle of the night.

31

Just like that. Go where they want. Whoopee!" He lay on his back and kicked his feet in the air.

"Okeydokee!" Faustina squealed till she had no more breath.

"Shut up!" I gave a great shout, louder than both of them. When they quieted down, I pointed out the window. "You see out there, far, far away out there." They both crawled across their beds and looked out in the night.

"What is?" asked Faustina.

"You mean the mountains?" said Pedro looking where I was pointing.

"Yes. The Mountains. The Sangre de Cristo. You know what's in those mountains?"

"Clouds," said Faustina.

"Don't be crazy," Pedro told her. "Clouds in the mountains! Clouds are in the sky."

"They come from the mountains. I see them every day, every day, every day."

"You're crazy every day." Pedro tried to stop her.

I stopped Pedro. "I'll tell you what's in those mountains. The biggest fish anywhere, and when they're cooked they taste like the best salted peanuts together with roasted marshmallows. And the best hunting, wild turkeys and bears to shoot at. And camping out every day. And every night getting up whenever you feel like it. And cooking whatever you want to eat."

"*Sopaipillas* with jelly?" These were sort of a puffed-up

kind of biscuits and they were what Faustina liked best.

"Yes," I told her.

"What else?" she asked.

"Up there are pools to swim in, with waterfalls coming down that you can slide in like a sled going down hill in the winter. Only to slide down in the water into a big pool is forty times better. Up there is never hot in the summer. On the very top of each mountain there is snow, like it was a big bunch of ice cream piled up."

"What flavor?" asked Faustina. "Chocolate?"

"No flavor."

"How does it taste then?"

"It tastes cool."

"That's all?"

"That's all."

"Okay," said Faustina.

"What else?" said Pedro.

"And up there are no mountains higher than where you are. When you look up, all you see is the sky. And the air is so clear every breath makes you fill up like a balloon. And when you look down you see everything. The whole Rio Grande Valley, almost the whole of all of New Mexico. No one can see more, or feel better than up there."

Faustina and Pedro kept looking at me even though I stopped talking and the only noise was Cyclone barking, out there where the family was with the new lamb.

"What else?" said Pedro.

"What else can there be? That's everything."

"So?" Pedro looked at me. "What's about it?"

Now was the time. For many years it had been a secret that I kept only to myself. A secret of only one person after a while gets too hard to keep. To make it real you have to tell someone else, even though they laugh at you, you've got to tell. Otherwise, all you got left is just one small, dried-up secret that's not worth anything.

"I'm going up there."

"To the Sangre de Cristo?"

"Yes."

"Okay," said Faustina. And she started to crawl back to her pillow.

"Sure," said Pedro. "Someday. We all go."

"Not someday. I go with the others this year. This here year!"

They both stopped from getting under the covers and looked at me. They didn't laugh.

"How do you know?" asked Faustina.

"I will arrange it myself."

"Arrange. That's not the way." Pedro shook his head. "First you got to know how to do everything. Then when you get into high school, or sometime like that, then it happens."

"Sure," said Faustina as if she knew what was all about.

"It never happens when anyone is so little like us," Pedro said.

"Like who?"

"Us."

"That's you," I told him. "Us—that's not me. You and Faustina are us. But me—I'm Miguel. And what I say is this. I'm going."

"How?"

What could I say? I said, "I have made a plan."

This was a big surprise to them both. They looked at me like I just grew wings.

"Your own plan?" Pedro crawled back to the side of the bed. I nodded my head, yes. "Like what?"

What could I say? I said, "A first-class plan. But I can't tell you about it. You'll see how it works."

"When?" yelled Faustina. "How soon? When can we see?"

"It starts tomorrow."

"Tomorrow!" Pedro yelled, too. With no one in the house, there was no reason not to make noise. "Tomorrow begins the plan? And you know how it all works, everything?"

"Everything."

"Wango!" Pedro made like he was throwing rocks all over the bedroom, he was so excited. "This is better than anything. This is as good like when we got the new tractor!"

"Okay," Faustina squealed. "Okeydokee!"

I laughed and yelled, too. It got so I thought I did have a plan, a real, good one. And everything was fixed so it would be all right now. We had a good time making a lot

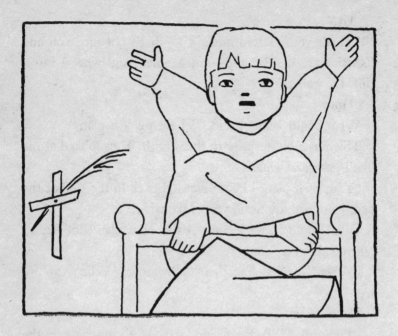

of noise. Pedro climbed up the back of the bed, the iron part where there are bumps and flowers.

"Look at me! I'm Miguel. I'm way up high. Miguel standing right on top of the mountains."

"I just remembered," yelled Faustina.

"What?"

"I'm thirsty."

I went and got her a glass of water from the kitchen. Then I put out the lights and undressed and got into bed.

In the quiet, I remembered. I didn't have any plan. In the quiet I heard them beyond the corral, Cyclone barking and the lamb making its kind of noise and the ewe making her kind of noise. All I could do was listen.

But even so, it was good. I had explained the secret. I had come out, like from behind the bushes when we play The Bandits Robbing Schaeffer's Drugstore, which is a drug store in Taos and a game we play at school. I had come out from behind the bushes and that meant, at least, that something had begun. And now that it had begun, I took one good look at the mountains through the window and then I went to sleep.

CHAPTER 4

IT is very interesting to watch a lamb, how it is born.

It is not difficult to get to see. Because a little while before it is the time for the birth the mother sheep, which is the ewe, begins to act a little strange.

Most of the time a ewe does not act like anything very much. It must be said, to begin with, that a ewe is not very smart. It knows to eat all the time, which is good enough. But that's about all. When it looks at you it is with the eyes of someone who does not understand, absolutely, even one word that you are saying. Not that I think a sheep should

38

understand words. It's just to explain what an empty look they go around with all the time.

But an hour or so before she gives birth, a ewe seems to get interested in something else than just eating, eating all the time. She goes all over the field looking as if for some place to lie down. First she smells here and turns around in a circle. And then she does the same thing all over again ten feet away. Often she even lies down for a second or two to try one place out. But it never seems to suit.

When it comes time for the birth she just lays down in any old place.

Then happens a remarkable thing. The ewe grunts and pushes. Not that she pushes anything, like a gate or a log. She just pushes inside herself. And makes this grunting noise. Now and again, she lifts her head from the ground and looks around at the back end of herself, as interested to see what is happening as I, who am watching.

At such a time, the ewe has a different look in her face. Her eyes are not empty. For once they look smart, like for instance the ewe was an old man who knew how everything should be and was standing off to one side watching it should happen right and in order. At such a time, the face of a ewe looks fine.

And then from the back end, peeping out, slowly, comes an airplane. That's what it looks like. The nose of an airplane which is all made out of glass, where the pilot sits, or maybe it's the bomber. And as it comes, if you look hard, you can see the pilot behind the round glass, his nose and his eyes and mouth. Only it's the lamb. And pretty soon you see the whole head of the lamb, even his ears. Only he is not like the pilot busy with switches and sticks, he just lays there taking it easy while the ewe grunts and pushes and keeps looking around to see if everything is going good.

By the time the front legs come out, it doesn't look like an airplane anymore. The round glass doesn't stay solid. It kind of busts up, and the lamb looks like it was all wrapped in one of those glass paper bags that you get with potato chips. Only this one is very clean with no printing on it, or pictures. And when the ewe gives a whole new set of grunts, and one big heave, and the back legs and tail and the whole lamb comes out, right that second you can say that the lamb is born.

It just lays on the grass, doing nothing in particular, all huddled up and shivering a little bit as if it was cold. And the ewe too lays her head on the ground for a little while, as if she was resting. The smart look on her face goes away and the regular empty look comes back, and right then she starts to lick. Lick, lick, licking at nothing, just the air. You see why in a couple of seconds when she gets up and lick, lick, licking, she turns around to the lamb on the ground and finally the licking and the lamb comes together. She licks the lamb all over, cleaning away what's left of the glass paper bag, and leaving the little one all nice and clean like it was a squeeze of toothpaste sitting on your brush in the morning when you scrub your teeth.

The lamb just doesn't lay there doing nothing in particular

for very long. It's not lazy. Very quick, even while the mother is licking it, it starts to move back and forth. Believe it or not, the lamb is trying to get up. Not ten minutes after it is born it wants to be up on its legs. I remember when Faustina was born all she did was lay around the house for weeks without doing anything except crying once in a while. She was pretty good at that. But a lamb wants to try walking right away.

The ewe can't help very much. What she does is to kind of scratch at the ground, first with one foot, then with the other. Why? I don't know. It doesn't help the baby get up. Maybe it shows the new one how to move its legs or something. Anyway, that's what the ewe does. And in a little bit the lamb makes it. He swings up and stands for a second or so like he was on stilts trying to get his balance. And the first couple of times it never seems to work. He always goes *borracho* and falls down in a heap.

He looks funny when he does stay up. Like a high chair. Nothing but four legs. His coat is all close and curly and sort of yellowish or brown. It takes days before it turns white. And he walks around like the ground beneath him was one big bowl of jelly. Less than an hour after the whole thing starts, there he goes, he and his mother ewe parading off like she was going to town to shop for the groceries. And by then, sure enough, the lamb is hungry. He goes nosing around underneath the ewe looking for his milk, like a calf with its cow or any animal with its mother, so that he ends up being real busy not one hour after he's born. A lot busier,

41

anyway, than Faustina ever was. Or any of the rest of us, I guess.

After the first lamb came, it happened like this twenty or thirty times a day, all day and all night. Wherever you looked it seemed as if a new lamb was on its way.

And each new one was hungry and it was cold. The hungry part, if nothing is wrong, the ewe takes care of. But there's not too much she can do for the cold, except to lick the lamb dry. If the lamb gets real cold, that's dangerous. It comes to be, like we say, chilled down, and has to be wrapped up and put near the fire and maybe fed some kind of medicine or a little whiskey. Because otherwise it would die.

That's when it happens. All the yelling. For wood to burn and water to boil, and bags and medicine so that Pedro or me, or anyone who is around goes running to bring what is asked, without any thank you or even a look to see who we are.

When this happened before it was bad.

But now it was twice as bad. Because for a day or two after the first lamb came, Pedro and Faustina watched me whatever I did to see how my plan was working. And, to be sure, I didn't have any plan. So that when everything happened just as in the years past, Pedro and Faustina were surprised.

You can imagine how I felt.

What's worse, the two of them followed me around wherever I went so that I couldn't forget I was supposed to have a plan, which after a while I would have liked to forget. One time I would be carrying a whole pitchfork of alfalfa to the drop bunch in the corral. The drop bunch are those ewes that are just about to give birth to their lambs and we keep collecting these ewes together so they can be watched when the time comes. And there I am with this big pile of alfalfa on the fork over my head, and Faustina grabs me by the elbow. When I turn around, all she does is to start winking at me in a secret way, winking as fast as she can, like a firefly.

"What's the matter?" I ask her.

"Goes good, hey?"

"What's good?"

And then I have to bend down for her to whisper in my ear. "Good plan, hey?"

"Sure, fine," I have to say. And then I go off with the alfalfa, feeling pretty bad because, first, it's a lie, and second, what's the lie getting me anyway?

Or I'm carrying a couple of heavy bucketfuls of cotton-seed cake, which is a kind of feed pressed together in little hard rolls that the ewes eat up as if it was chocolate-covered marshmallows. And as if it wasn't bad enough carrying two heavy buckets, Pedro gets in my way.

"What happens?" he asks.

"Where?" I ask him.

"When do we see it? The plan?"

What is there for me to say? So I say, "It happens now. Right now."

"No!" He's real surprised.

"Yes."

"To me, looks like you're just carrying a couple of buckets of cake."

"Maybe that's what it looks like to you but all this, it's part of it."

"No! I can't hardly believe it!"

"That's because you don't know how the plan works."

"Sure is a fine plan. So secret you can't even tell when it's happening."

"Yeah."

"I wish I'd thought of it," says Pedro, and how do you think that makes me feel? I feel like there was a war and I was a traitor, except that even a traitor goes around fooling people for some kind of reason. And here I was without any reason at all.

After a couple of days Faustina forgot all about the plan because she don't remember anything too good for very long, no matter what it is.

But not Pedro. He would never leave off asking me, "Is this it? Is that it?" And sometimes I would say yes and sometimes no, depending on nothing except which word came into my head first. I would have given him something, like my Indian stone, if he would forget the whole thing. But how could I even talk to him about making any kind of a swap? All I could do was hope he'd forget. But not Pedro. He's got a memory like four horses.

Every night when we got into bed he would ask me if

the plan goes good that day or not. And if I told him it goes good, I'd feel how he shook his head at how smart I was. He'd be glad about it. So most of the time I told him it goes good. If it made him feel glad, why not? I would just as soon see somebody get something out of all this, whatever it was.

But no matter how Pedro felt, or I felt, or what I told him, one thing was for sure. It wasn't going any better this year than last. And it was no use making believe. I had to figure something out, or I had to tell Pedro the truth. One or the other.

I studied about it for a couple of days, and then I found an idea. It wasn't a great secret plan like Pedro thought I was working, but it was something. I did it with Grandpa's help. I got the job of branding the sheep with numbers.

The reason why there has to be numbers, is because the ewe stops being so smart after the lamb is born. And the lamb is not old enough to have any brains at all, even if it was going to get some later on. So that if one loses the other, the ewe and the lamb both have a hard time knowing what to do about it.

If they stay apart too long, it gets serious. The ewe won't recognize her lamb at all after a while. And then she won't feed the lamb as her child even if you bring the lamb back to her. This makes for one whole lot of trouble.

That's why you can't let them stay apart, a ewe and its lamb. The only thing is, it is not so easy to tell who belongs to who. It's a problem with ewes because they all look alike,

45

and that's a problem with lambs, too. No one looks any more different from any other than a handful of peanuts.

To get over this problem we put, with a branding iron, a number on the ewe right after she gives birth and the same number on the lamb. Only we don't brand them by burning like they do with cattle, only with paint. There's a bucket of black paint and ten irons which have at the end the figure of a number, like 1, and 2, 3, 4 and so on up to 9. There is no 10, only a 0. The way you make 10 is you take the iron with 1 and the iron with 0 and first put on one then the other. This way you can make any number you like. Four Hundred Sixty Two, for instance, 462, or even seventeen million five hundred and sixty thousand if you wanted to, I guess, and you had a sheep long enough.

It's a special kind of paint, and you put it right on the wool of the lamb and the ewe where it stays and doesn't come off, even in the rain. It doesn't hurt the animal, at all. And once you put the numbers on them, then you don't have any trouble. If you see a lamb wandering around all by itself looking not so happy, which is a pretty easy way for a lamb to look, you just see what is its number. And if it's, for instance, 462, then you search around until you find the ewe with 462. You bring the lamb to the ewe. They get together. And that's that.

The first lamb, the one I never did get out to see that night, was marked with its mother 1. The next pair 2, and so on. By the time it got up to forty or so, I figured out

this idea. Instead of just being around to run and get things when someone asked, if I could get a regular job that would be much, much better. That would put me way ahead of where I was last year. Grandpa had the paint pot with the numbers, and he was doing the branding. I asked if he would show me how and if he would let me do it.

He asked me if I could count and fast as I could I counted up and up and up until I lost my breath. At counting I'm all right, and I always get stars in arithmetic. Grandpa thought I was a good counter, too, so he showed me how the job was done.

It was not so hard at all. You take which ever number

you want and just dip it, not all the way in, only on the top of the paint. Then while somebody holds the ewe you just touch the iron to the wool coat on the side, not too hard. The reason why not too hard has nothing to do with hurting the ewe, it can't hurt anyway. It's because if you push too hard you push a lot of wool together with the number, and when you take the iron away all the wool with the paint spreads out and instead of a number all you've got is a splotch like you were eating raspberry jam and it got on your face. And this don't help at all. With the lamb you can press hard because the wool is so short, little curly hair, and it takes the number fine.

The hardest thing is not how you hold the iron or anything like that, but how you keep the numbers in your head. Like when you might just brand a ewe and a lamb one hundred and seventy-three, and then another one doesn't come for an hour or maybe longer, you've got to remember that the next number is one hundred seventy-four. If you put the same number twice, on two different families, then you've got trouble. So most of the time after I got started I'd be going around all the time saying numbers to myself, like One Eighty Six, One Eighty Six, One Eighty Six, so as not to forget that it was the next number. Remembering, that was the hardest part.

But, as far as my idea went, remembering was the best part, the very best part, too. On account of, no one knew the next number but me. My father might come with one ewe and a lamb and he would hold them while I put on

186. Then later Blasito would come with another ewe and lamb. But he wouldn't know the number. Only I would—187. Even if he took the pot of paint and the irons himself, it wouldn't do him any good. He wouldn't know what number to make unless I was there to tell him—187.

So all the time the men were working you would hear them, the way they would call.

"Ai Miguel—bring the irons."

"Next, Miguel—over here!"

"Where's Miguel? Where's the bookkeeper?" That was Eli, who made a joke by calling me the bookkeeper because I was always so busy making numbers and saying numbers to myself. It was a joke and everybody laughed. I laughed too. Because of the way that it was going so good.

When we went out in the morning we would all walk together, each one carrying his tools, like a sheep hook, or a pair of shearing clippers, or a rope and a pitchfork, and I would carry my pot of paint and numbers along with the others. It is still cold as the day gets light. We would stand for a little by the fence of the corral, and the men would talk and finish their cigarettes. And I would say something too, like, "This morning is colder than was yesterday morning," or, "The sheep are quiet, they have had a good night." Sometimes one of the men would answer me, saying, "Yes," or, "That's right, Miguel."

And then someone would say, "*Vamonos*—let's go" and we would all go to work. What I mean is, me along with everybody else.

49

This was better than last year, or any year before. Much better. This was fine.

And Pedro! How he used to watch me! Big eyes. Wherever I went, looking to see what I did. About Pedro, I felt better now. Because it wasn't such a lie any more in my own mind, the plan.

Now when he would come up to me on the side and say quiet, "Everything all right, heh? Real good?"

Then I could say, "Not bad."

And the only thing that was not true was the way I said it, like everything was nothing so much, and as if all along I figured it out so it would happen just this way. That wasn't so much of a lie.

With everything else working out so good this year, I could stand that much of a lie anyway.

CHAPTER 5

BUT there was something else about the time I worked
with the numbers.

This part is a little hard to say. It was good that I was
a part of all the work, and everyone knew that it was me,
Miguel. And it was good, too, I didn't have to fool Pedro
anymore. All this was good.

But the something else is this. It would get so sometimes
that I would forget what the good of it was. I mean the
good that it was for me. Or even that what was happening
was me, Miguel, doing what had to be done for myself.

And all that was left was the sheep and what they had to have. Like the sun they needed to keep warm. And the rain and the green grass to feed them. In the same way they needed someone to work and keep them all as a family together and healthy. They had nothing else except the sun and the rain and the grass and you.

And the numbers.

Without numbers, there would be many lambs alone. And a lamb, by itself, one small one looking around at the others, frightened maybe because it was going to die— this is a thing you do not forget.

"That is the real work of a pas*tor*," my grandfather told me, "of a shepherd. To see that in all the flock there is no one that is alone by himself. Everyone together. Only so can all live."

"How is it they go off, the way they do, by themselves?" I asked. "Why are sheep not so smart?"

"Sheep! There are many men who don't understand this simple thing. Not only sheep."

"You get the bookkeeper all mixed up?" Eli came to us with a ewe and a lamb to be numbered. He laughed at Grandpa, who sometimes we call the Father of the Chavez. "Talking about men, Padre de Chavez, together with sheep, you make Miguel dizzy, putting everything in one pot."

Eli carried the lamb by the hind legs with its head hanging down. They don't seem to mind, the lambs, they even look comfortable this way. The ewe he brought along by sitting on her back and pushing with his feet. This way, holding with your knees, the ewe can't get away and you can shove her, if you're big enough, in which direction you want. Eli held them, first the ewe then the lamb, while I put on them the number 188.

"Your grandfather," Eli talked to me while I worked, "he's very wise. So wise he can say eight things with one word. And after two glasses of wine he can say eight things without even one word, just by waving his hand. No, Padre?"

My grandfather laughed and he gave Eli a little push in the face. Then Eli laughed.

"It's simple," he turned back to me, "Men are not so smart because they are lazy. Sheep are not so smart because they are sheep. For the first days a ewe cannot even tell her own lamb by looking at it. Only by smelling, very close. So if the lamb is on the wrong side of the wind, even a few feet away, they don't know each other. Over there!" he pointed to the other side of the corral. "One sixty four, over there, the lamb."

There was one lamb, with the big number on its side, standing high on its legs, looking all around and yelling like the whole world was on fire. And there, not many feet away, was a ewe standing straight up with a stiff neck, looking like someone had just called her a dirty name and grunting so loud almost she sounded like the fire siren over in Taos. On her side, too, was the number 164.

They looked right at each other, one bawling and the

other like a siren. The two of them with 164. Nothing happened. They just kept making noise. Then the lamb rushed off in one direction, running everywhere in the flock like a player in a football game. And the ewe walked off proud in the other direction, smelling every lamb she came to, baaing all the time, like she was looking for a policeman to complain. The lamb had a hard time to keep his feet, falling over every little pebble. He stumbled around trying to get underneath the ewes with all the wrong numbers, 114, and 73, 152 and even the ewe I just put the number on, 188.

"Go ahead," Grandpa told me.

"Fix 'em up," said Eli.

I went over and grabbed the lamb, it took me two tries because they always run away, and carried him over to the ewe. When I came close, the ewe started to back away, thinking I was trying to catch her. But then when I got close enough for her to smell the lamb and put it down beside her, bang—you think it was the last day at school, the way everything got so excited. The ewe bellowing and the lamb yowling, and the ewe smelling the back end of the lamb to make sure there was no mistake, and the lamb crowding around underneath so he can find a nipple and start eating. When he did, he backed away a little, then in he went like the ewe was a bank on the side of the road and he was a bull dozer, bump, push, bump. This was to loosen up the milk, Eli told me, so it would come easier.

But always it is not so simple. Even when the ewe and

the lamb do get together there may be trouble because of the way the wool grows on the big sheep, so thick that the lamb can't get at the nipple to suck good. Then what is needed is for my father to clip away all the wool from underneath the ewe with the big shears that he has. Once that is done, there's no trouble at all. No matter where the lamb goes under there, since there are two different nipples, he finds something to eat.

Unless, of course, the ewe doesn't want the lamb around at all.

I asked why that should be. "Isn't this what is best for the ewe," I asked, "to have for itself a lamb?"

"Without doubt," said my grandfather. "Yet also with men sometimes they don't always do what they know is best."

"Pardon me," Eli was laughing again. "What you tell the boy, Padre mio, is all clouds and wind. There are reasons, Miguel, it may be one of many reasons. Perhaps the ewe had a hard time having the lamb born and it hurt her, and she wants to get away from what hurt her. Or maybe the way the lamb feeds may give her, at the beginning, a little pain. Or maybe she is a yearling, a ewe in her first year who is having her first lamb, and she doesn't know what is expected. All sorts of reasons. When anything like this happens, then it is necessary for us to help them, like we say, to mother them up, the ewe and the lamb."

"As Gabriel does now." Grandpa pointed to my big brother on the other side of the fence.

What Gabriel was doing right then was trying to catch a ewe, to cut it out of a bunch of sheep, with a sheep hook. This is a long pole with a metal thing at the end that is shaped like what you see sometimes in printing—?, a question mark. Where it curls around up there and comes to an end, that part is just so narrow it can slip past the ankle of the hind foot of the sheep. Where it goes around wide up at the top it's not so wide as to be bigger than the hoof of the sheep, so once you slip the hook over the ankle the ewe can't get her foot out and she's caught. Sometimes it is called a crook, this kind of pole, and it's fun to use like going fishing—though not for the sheep, I guess, they always set up such a holler when they're caught.

When Gabriel caught the ewe now, number 182, my biggest brother Blasito came with the lamb of the same number. And while Gabby turned the ewe over, like she was sitting up, Blasito held the lamb down to where it should eat and milked the ewe a little right in to the lamb's mouth. This got the lamb excited because it tasted so good, and my brothers let the lamb suck for a while holding the ewe so it couldn't get away.

"Sometimes that's enough to bring them together," said Eli. And indeed, so it looked when they let the ewe go. The lamb kept right after it, pushing away to get its dinner. "Now that the mother is a little used to it, and the baby knows how to manage, he won't let the mother get far away from him."

"But the shepherd must watch," my grandfather warned me, "he must never stop watching."

"That's right." Eli agreed with him. "Often that's not enough to bring them together."

"And if he doesn't take care," said Grandfather, "and do whatever else is necessary, and the ewe and the child go apart from each other, that's a sin."

"A sin?" I thought you could only have a sin when it had something to do with church or saying your prayers.

"Why do you talk about a sin?" Eli wanted to know. "What's the sin about it?"

"The boy should know this." Grandpa was a little mad at Eli. "Whenever something grows and you keep it from growing anymore, that's a sin. And if it's a life, living, and you let it to die, that's a sin."

"Pardon me," said Eli. "You fill up the bookkeeper's head like a hay wagon. What else should he know but this is the work we do, we raise wool and lambs. If a ewe sickens and dies we lose the wool. And if a lamb is lost we have one less to take to market. And for those that die all the work we've done to raise them is wasted, and for the hours and days we put in we don't make wages. Why talk about sin? This is our job. For this we get paid. Dollars and cents. That's all."

"My little Eli." Grandpa made noises at my big uncle like he was a baby, like Faustina in the cradle. "What a smart little one is Eli."

And then he started to talk to Eli in Spanish, fast, with a very stern face, but I don't know if he was angry at Eli or making fun of him because to such a big man as Eli he talked as if he were only a little boy playing on the floor.

And what he told Eli was that it was he, my grandfather, who started this flock, which was true. It had happened very long ago when he was a young man, Grandfather, no older than Gabriel. Until Grandfather's time, all the men of the Chavez family had only worked, like having a job, as shepherds. They worked for other men who owned flocks of thousands and tens of thousands of sheep, and who owned land that stretched as far as one could see. They were called *patrons*, these very rich men who owned sheep, and they had working for them many, many shepherds.

But my grandfather, for his work he took sheep instead of wages. This was a way of working called *partido*. It was arranged that the *patron* would give my grandfather so many sheep, and Grandpa would take care of them on the land of his boss for the whole year. At the end of the year, he would give back to the *patron* all the sheep he received in the beginning and one third of all the lambs that were born. All the rest of the lambs, for salary, he would keep for himself.

It sounded like a good way. But it was hard. First, the shepherd—the *partidero*—would have to borrow from the *patron* so that he could have food for the year. And if any sheep were lost, he would have to make it up to the *patron* out of the lambs he earned. Most of the time it did not

58

work out so good. The shepherd ended up with very few lambs and owing the *patron* many weeks and even years of work ahead.

One had to be very lucky, or work very hard, to make out all right.

"It was true I was lucky," Grandfather shook his fist at Eli. "But it was work, too. Me, alone, without cousins and uncles or you and the other boys. If it was for money alone, I would have taken wages. And I would have had a good time going into town without thinking of anything else. This is the way you live, making money. But in those days long ago, it was not for money that I worked, and to have sheep now is not only money. It is a proper way for a man to live in the world, with sheep, taking care of them so that all can live under heaven, you and the sheep both. If this was not so, my smart little one, Eli, we would not be working here today with our own flock. Understand!"

"All right," Eli didn't look as if Grandpa was angry at him, he smiled. "I give up."

"You don't have to give up," said Grandpa. "Only when you explain to the boy, explain right."

But Eli didn't have a chance anymore, because someone yelled "Number!" It was my other uncle, Bonifacio. "Miguel, here with the irons."

I went over and put very carefully the number 189 on the ewe Bonifacio was holding, and then on the lamb. After I finished, he tied with a rope the hind leg of the ewe with the hind leg of the lamb. When he saw me watching he said, "That's because the ewe doesn't want to nurse the lamb. She runs away. Now she can't."

"I know," I said. "I heard all about."

"Everything? Already you're a first class pas*tor*?"

"Well, almost everything."

"Then let me tell you, to tie them together this way is good only in the corral. It is no good when you are driving the flock out on the range. Because there the rope gets all tangled up in a bush, maybe, or around a rock, and the two of them get caught and can't move."

"That would be the end for them, huh?"

"If they couldn't move to eat and drink," Bonifacio picked up his sheep hook. "Or if a coyote came along."

"It would be a sin?"

He looked back at me. "Who you been talking to, Grandpa?"

"Yes," I said.

"Then you don't need me to answer questions. You just listen to him."

I never got to know who was right, Uncle Eli or Grandfather Chavez. But this I knew. To leave even one lamb outside the flock, whether it was a sin or just a good way to lose dollars and cents, that was the worst that could happen. And the best of all the different ways to get a lamb and a ewe to be mothered-up, my father told me, was the lambing pens.

These were built all over, in the corners of the corrals or any place. In the corner you would put up some planks and block off a place just big enough for a sheep. In this space you would put the ewe and the lamb, and leave them for a day or even longer. During this time the ewe can't run away and in the end the mother and the lamb get to know each other good and like each other. Then there is no more danger letting them go off by themselves. There was more than a dozen of these lambing pens all around, and they were always filled up with a family that was settling down to live together.

So that at the last, whether with lambing pens or by one of the other ways, the whole flock was taken care of and everybody was happy.

Except for the orphans.

I don't care how good you are thinking up things that are sad, there is nothing sadder than a lamb that is an orphan.

We call them tramps, such an orphan, but it isn't their fault like they ran away from home or something. It isn't even because the mother dies, most of the time. An orphan comes most of the time when there are twins, and the mother, she does not have enough milk to feed both. Or when a lamb gets lost from its mother for two or three days, and she doesn't recognize it even by the smell anymore. This doesn't have to be our fault or anybody's fault. It could be there's a storm and the sheep get separated, or they're frightened by a wolf or another kind of animal and they go rushing around.

But however it happens an orphan is one unlucky animal.

And the reason for this is that a ewe will have nothing to do absolutely with any lamb except her own lamb, she won't feed it or lick it or anything. What's worse, when the orphan comes hanging around looking for a meal, nosing this way and that to see what he can get, the ewe beats him up bad. A ewe can butt almost as bad as a nanny goat. And when she takes off and bangs at one of these orphans that's trying to get friendly with her, it's like the orphan got hit by a truck.

We had two of them this year. And for a little while we let the orphans hang around to give them a chance, in case we made some kind of mistake, to find their mothers by themselves. But they never did. They were like a couple of big zeros, going this way and that way in the middle of a lot of numbers that were happy together in pairs, two 1s, two 2s, two 3s, all the way up into the hundreds. All the orphans got all day long was ewes butting them from the right and the left until you'd think they were black and blue, only lambs don't get black and blue, just dirty.

But then it happened that one of the lambs which did have a mother died. This was bad, without doubt. But it gave my father a chance to fix up at least one of the orphans with a mother.

The way he did this was kind of a trick. He got the dead lamb—its number was 86—from where it was laying on the ground at the feet of the ewe that was its mother. The ewe just stood there hour after hour, baaing and bleating because the lamb wouldn't get up and feed itself and go walking around with her like he did before he died. My father took the body of the lamb around to the other side of the shearing shed where the ewe couldn't see. And here he stripped off its coat with a hunting knife. Then he fitted the little sheepskin of the dead lamb over one of the orphans. It didn't fit so good, about the way one of my father's coats fit me, but at least it stayed on the lamb and gave it a number, 86.

"When the ewe smells the skin of her own dead lamb," my father looked up to me watching him work, "she'll think the orphan is her child, and she'll let the orphan feed and stay together with her as a family."

"It's like a trick?"

My father, working, shook his head, yes.

"Is it right? I mean to do it?"

"Is what right?"

"To fool the ewe."

"Me?"

"Well, what I want to say is, yes—you."

He stood up with the orphan in his arms and shook his head. "When anyone must believe something the way a ewe must believe she has a child, you don't fool her when you help. Watch!"

When he went around back to the ewe with the orphan, the sheepskin hanging on it with the number 86, it was interesting. First the ewe looked suspicious at the orphan standing there, then it sniffed a little in front and behind, then it went off and turned around and came back. The orphan didn't do anything. I guess it was so beat up trying to be friendly with ewes, it was scared to do anything. It just stood there like, wrapped around in a blanket with the number 86 on it. Then the ewe gave a different kind of a cry, happy, and shoved the orphan with its nose. This was some kind of signal. The orphan went right for its dinner, and the ewe looked down as if this was the smartest thing anybody ever did, looking proud as a queen.

"See?" said my father.

"I see."

They walked off together, the ewe number 86 and the lamb with the coat 86 dragging by one corner on the ground.

"The ewe is happy," said my father. "It believes it has a lamb. And the lamb is happy, it believes it has a mother. And this is what they must believe if they are to live happy. This is not fooling anybody."

I said, "I think so."

"And in a day or two it will be true, without doubt. Soon the smell of the skin from the dead lamb goes away. At the same time, the ewe gets used to the smell, the real smell, of the orphan. She will recognize the new smell to be the smell of her child. When that happens we will take the sheep skin off the lamb. You will put 86 on this lamb to match its new mother and they will be a ewe and a lamb together."

"I'll watch out," I said, "and have the irons ready. The 8 and the 6."

But thank goodness not so many lambs die, not enough so you can work this trick for all the orphans. We couldn't do it this year for even the second orphan.

This one was given to my older sisters, Tomasita and Leocadia, to keep. Between them the girls had five orphans to take care of last year. They fed each one milk out of a beer bottle with a nipple on it. Then after a while they showed the orphans how to eat grass and alfalfa from around the farm. My sisters did all right. At the end of the summer they sold the lambs they raised and made much, much money. Fifteen dollars for each one.

The orphan they have now they call Jimmy. He is like a pet for my sisters, walking behind them wherever they go.

This is the way it is with lambs, if they don't have a ewe they'll follow anything around. Once I heard a poem called "Mary had a little lamb." I don't know whether it is a good poem or a bad poem. But it's true, I know that. The way the lamb followed this girl Mary when she went to school, that's the way it happens. Not only does a lamb follow someone called Mary around, but even a truck or a tractor or, if nothing else, an old tire that Pedro might be rolling along.

To be taken care of by my sisters an orphan is at least lucky. He won't die. But he can't be very happy. He never becomes part of the regular flock. He's always off by himself. What's more he stays with the girls on the farm all summer. He never goes with the flock when it leaves for summer pasture. He never climbs with the rest when they go up there, up into the Mountains of the Sangre de Cristo.

Unless I put on him a number, one that matches the number of a ewe, one of the numbers that is part of the flock, he gets left behind.

You can see how all I had in my head these days was numbers. And to see that no one got left out, and to put numbers on them. Eights and twos and sixes and threes. Numbers all day long. And even when I got into bed at night and I would answer Pedro's questions and tell him that the plan was going pretty good, even then I couldn't forget numbers. And numbers would be still in my head, the very last thing when I would take a look at the mountains before turning over.

Once I even thought I saw up there, on the Sangre de Cristo, it must have been a shadow or something from a cloud, but anyway, I thought I saw up on the mountains the number, 12. And I too was, 12.

I went to sleep thinking that it was all right now, the mountain and I, we were like mothered-up.

CHAPTER 6

AND then it was all over.

Comes eight hundred ninety-two—eight hundred ninety-three—eight hundred ninety-four, and that is the last of the new lambs. No more numbers.

This happened in the first week of May, when I put the number 894 on the very last lamb to be born and on its mother, the ewe. After that I was no longer, like what Uncle Eli called me, a bookkeeper. That part was finished.

My father told me to clean the irons with turpentine, to wash off the paint and the dirt and stuff that had got stuck to them and to wrap them up in a rag for next year. What Uncle Eli said now was, "Miguel, looks like you're out of business." I guess I was.

And all that was left was me and Pedro and Faustina going to school at eight o'clock every morning with our books, and coming home in the afternoon with maybe a couple of new stars. The men were busy, my father and my uncles, spreading the flock out in bunches on the pueblo land nearest the farm in order to feed all the new mothers the fresh green grass that was coming up. And when my brothers Blasito and Gabriel came home from high school in the afternoon they would be busy with the tractor, plowing up the fields and getting ready to plant alfalfa. And even Leocadia and Tomasita were busy with Jimmy the orphan when they weren't helping my mother in the house.

All that was left was me and Pedro sitting on a fence, watching it all, and Pedro asking me, "This is part of it, too, the plan?"

And I'd say, "Yes."

And he'd say, "My, you'd never believe it."

It was almost like it never happened, the time when I could feel good with Pedro and be almost one hundred per cent honest with him. And the mornings when I'd walk out with the men, me carrying the irons and the paint and they carrying the rest of the stuff, and standing around while they finished their cigarettes, talking things over. All that was now like it never happened.

Now was worse than just no good. Because wanting to go up into the mountains is not like wanting someday to be a policeman or an airplane pilot. You can forget about policemen and airplanes for a little while, for an hour or for fifteen minutes. But the mountains of the Sangre de Cristo, they were always there. No matter where you looked. Every time you took your eyes off the ground. There they were, far away.

Something had to keep happening to remind my father and grandfather and uncles how easy it was for me, Miguel, to be part of everybody busy with the flock.

I was lucky. It did happen.

It was on account of the storms.

Where we live we have many storms during the winter, with much snow, and ice on the river, the Rio Pueblo, and hailstones bigger than cubes of sugar, only round the way hailstones are. No matter how bad are the storms, it is not too bad for the sheep on account of their wool. Indeed, the winter is even better than some other times on account of the sheep don't have to be herded to water, they eat the snow instead. And underneath the snow they find the grass.

But if more storms come in the late season, after the winter is over and the lambs are born, then it is very hard. With the lambs so young, some are not strong enough to keep warm and healthy in the big storms, and so they get sick sometimes, and even some can die.

This year there came many storms after the lambing, in the second week of May.

The storms came with a great wind that blew in from the deserts where live the Navajo Indians, Gabriel told me, wide places that stretch to the west across our state, which is New Mexico, and into Arizona, which is the state next to ours. And with the wind there was always much thunder. And everywhere you look, coming down all of a sudden across the sky like scratches, lightning—white scratches in the low clouds all around. The rain was cold, and soon everything was heavy with the rain—your clothes and the hay and the mud in the roads—so that you had to leave the truck stuck in the road and walk wherever you were going through the cold rain.

Everyone did what they could for the flock. It was split up into bunches of maybe two hundred sheep each, in order to take care of them better. Blasito had one bunch out with the sheep wagon. And Bonifacio had another bunch over on the mesa. Eli had some on his farm, and he put a stove in one shed where he took lambs who got more cold than the others. We had a bunch, too, at our place. And after the first day my mother always had two or three lambs keeping warm in a box next to the woodbox near the kitchen stove. Outside, each one of the men kept a big fire going every night so that their bunch would come around to get warm, so they wouldn't get split up and separated in the night.

On the morning of the third day it happened. I was out in the barnyard getting stovewood for breakfast, and I saw Blasito, my biggest brother, coming in on the horse, Blackie. Gabriel had gone out to take his place an hour before, and Blasito should have been glad to come in to the house to get good hot food to eat and dry clothes and a rest. But he didn't look glad, getting off the horse, not at all.

"Blasito," I yelled over to him, "how goes?"

He spit. And what he said in Spanish, if I ever said it I'd get plenty from my mother. Whatever it was that happened was bad, that was sure, because Blasito always looks like he enjoys himself, whether he's driving the school bus or anything, and mostly whatever happens he will smile.

"Blas!"

He just gave me one look like he was tired, but no answer;

and he went into the house. By the time I got the ten sticks of wood piled up on my arm, which is the number my mother and I have decided is one load, by the time I got into the house, everybody else knew except me.

They were all sitting around the table eating bacon and eggs and things, listening to Blas who sat there scratching his head with both hands, and they didn't even look around when I made a big noise dumping the wood into the box.

"There was nothing else to do," Blasito was saying. "When Gabby showed up with the horse, I circled way around to the south, toward Gijosa, on my way in here. And, well—nothing."

"How many do you think?" asked my father.

"Better than a dozen," Blasito started to eat his eggs. "I made a quick count this morning just as soon as it was light. You know how it is—to know exact, you can't. But at least a dozen."

There was just a second no one said anything, so I asked, "What happens?"

No one answered. My mother said, "Did you notice, were any stray lambs left behind?"

Blasito shrugged his shoulders while he ate. "I didn't wait to look."

"What is?" I asked.

"All that lightning," said Leocadia, "just before it was dawn. The thunder woke me. That's what did it. I was scared myself."

"Like I was saying," I said. "What is?"

"It won't be easy in all of this." Bonifacio was having coffee, and he lit a cigarette. "They'll hole up somewhere to get out of the weather, under rocks, out of sight."

"Yes," my father nodded. "No good."

"But look," I said. "Did something happen?"

"The worst of it is," Blasito stopped eating and started to scratch his head again. "I missed a shot at a coyote just yesterday, in the afternoon, about half a mile west of the wagon. And I don't think it was alone."

"There are many this year," said my mother. "More than I remember."

I slipped a little off my chair, and under the table I gave Pedro one big kick. He was looking from one to the other, his mouth open, as they talked. He turned quick.

"What?" I made like I was shouting but without giving a sound, just with my lips. "What?"

"Sheep," he talked to me in the same way, only making the words with his mouth. "Lost. Last night."

Ai, this was bad. More than a dozen sheep, and their lambs, to lose so many for us is a great loss.

"We'll drive the bunches together," my father was saying, "over to Eli's place. That'll give three of us a chance to search."

It was bad, I thought, listening to my father make plans to find the sheep, but in a different kind of way it could be for me, maybe, good. Because if I could go off with the men to find the sheep, and maybe I would be the one to find them, without doubt it would be a great thing and everyone would know it, even better than they knew about the numbers.

Besides, the truth is I'm a great finder. Because last year when I lost my Indian rock—which is just a stone with kind of a hole in it that the Indians used to use, my grandfather told me, to grind corn—when I lost that everyone said I'd never find it. And to be honest, I didn't think so myself. On account of where we live, in our country, if there's more of anything than anything else, it's rocks laying on the ground. That's why everyone said how could I expect to find one special one, and they told me to forget it. But I didn't. I was lucky and I found it. And everyone said I had a good way of finding things.

"Remember!" I nearly shouted, and my father stopped talking.

"About what?" he asked me.

"About my Indian stone, the one with the hole."

"Miguel, we're talking here about finding some sheep. Some sheep strayed last night, do you understand?"

"Yes, I know," I said. "That's why I'm telling you about the stone."

"What's the stone got to do with a bunch of lost ewes?"

"Nothing." What could I say? "Except everybody said it was no good looking for the stone. Remember?"

"Well, what good was it? The stone?" My father took a bite from a biscuit and kept chewing on it, looking at me.

"The good of the stone?" I don't know how it is that

things get turned around like this. "It was good for the Indians, I guess. They used it to grind corn."

"I'm glad it was good for the Indians." My father swallowed what he was chewing, and looked at my mother like it was her fault. "Sometimes I don't know what goes on here," he said.

And then he went on talking to Bonifacio and Blasito about bringing in the horses to saddle them; and Faustina, who was sitting on the other side of my mother, started to squeak and giggle.

"Miguel," she whispered. "He's babaloo." That was her new word, these days, babaloo.

And Pedro looked at me as if it was a big surprise.

The thing was I couldn't let this chance go!

"I can find them!" I said it right out loud. They stopped talking again, the men, to look at me. "I know I can find them. Or at least I can help."

"What time is school?" my father said to my mother. "Isn't it about time for them to take off?"

What was worse, the school bell started to ring, over in Los Cordovas, just then. And my mother, she pointed with her head for all of us to get our books.

"All I want to say," I started to explain to my father. But he smiled and shook his head.

"It's all right, Miguel. We'll find them. This is not a job for you. We'll have them here when you get back from school."

My mother smiled too, then, at my father. "Next time,"

she put her hand on the back of my head, "we'll let you find them all by yourself. But this once, come, on your way."

Faustina giggled again. "Babaloo—Mickey," she squeaked.

I got up and gave her nose a good pinch and beat it out of the house with my books, carrying my coat without even waiting to put it on.

So then, when Juby told me what he saw, you can imagine how important it was.

Juby is my oldest friend. He lives in Los Cordovas where the schoolhouse is. Ever since I can remember doing anything, fishing or playing ball or just talking, most of these things I did with Juby. And as long as I can remember Juby, he's been wearing this same big black hat with a wide brim on it curved up on the sides like the wings look on a buzzard when it circles around, taking things easy in the sky. By now the hat is pretty old and has some holes in it, but it still looks all right on Juby because it would be hard to tell what Juby looked like without it.

He was playing basketball when I came to the yard of the schoolhouse, Faustine and Pedro after me. That is, Juby and some of the others were playing just shooting for baskets, and as soon as he saw me, he waved his hand and quit, and came over.

"How're you doing?" he asked me.

I said, "Pretty good," because what's the use telling everybody your troubles?

"D'you folks lose any sheep," he asked me.

"What?" I made one grab at his arm and held tight.

"Sheep," he said. "What's the matter?"

"Now look, Juby," I said. "What's the use talking you and me? How do you know we got missing sheep? What about them?"

"I saw them."

"What?"

"At least I think they're yours. From the shape of the numbers they look like yours." We don't put our brand on the sheep until after we shear them. But our numbers had a different shape to them than any of the others in the neighborhood.

"Where?"

"Then you did lose some sheep?"

"Juby!" I was a little excited. "What's the use, Juby? Just to talk? Where did you see them?"

"Well—you know Carlotta?"

"Who?"

"Our milk cow."

"Cows? What about the sheep?"

"I'm telling you. She got loose last night, Carlotta, and when I went to herd her back I saw these sheep."

"Where? Where? Where?"

"What's the matter with you, Mike? Something wrong?"

"Juby," I said. "You and me, you're my oldest friend aren't you?"

"Sure."

"Then tell me, where are the sheep?"

"Give me a chance. I saw them across the river. Maybe fifteen, ewes and lambs. They looked like they were heading straight for Arroyo Hondo." It was just in the opposite direction from where Blasito and the sheep wagon was, from where he looked this morning. "Were they yours?"

"You don't know what this could mean, Juby. That is for me."

But just then the bell started to ring, and Mrs. Mertian, who is the teacher of our school over there in Los Cordovas, she came to the door and told everybody to come in.

"Let's go." Juby went with the others into the class.

And that's the way things stood.

On one side, Mrs. Mertian with the bell ringing. And on the other side the big mountains, looking very dark and a little mad, if you can think of mountains like they were mad. But that was the way they looked, and at that moment there came thunder from behind them.

And in the middle, I stood. If it ever happened that I came home with the missing sheep? Could anything ever be better?

Mrs. Mertian said, "Miguel."

From the Sangre de Cristo there came thunder, very low.

I did not stand too long. Because there was no question about it! Nothing, that is to say, nothing at all could ever be better.

I headed straight for the Boys on the other side of the yard.

"Miguel!" It was Mrs. Mertian yelling. I didn't even look back. I jumped into this whole bunch of bushes and started down the hill.

Big champion jumps, every one breaking a world's record, that's the way I came down that hill. With each jump, everything went flying. My books banging at the end of the rope in my hand, swinging all around. My arms, like I had a dozen of them, each one going off by itself. My feet, like I was on a bike, working away to keep my balance. But I couldn't balance. Except by jumping. I couldn't stop. Each jump bigger than the last. I cleared a bush, then a big cracked rock. Then, I wasn't going to make it but I did, a high cactus. Each jump I thought was the last. Each jump was going to end with a cracked head, a split rib, or maybe two broken legs. But it didn't. I don't know why? There was nothing I could do. I came down that hill, like a boulder bumping in bigger and bigger bumps, bumping its way down a cliff. Straight for the river. Until I wasn't scared of falling anymore. I had to fall! Or land in the river. But how? I grabbed a bush. That didn't stop me. And then my books caught, between a couple of rocks. I slipped, grabbed at another bush. Slid a couple of feet, and then took off again. And then I landed. On my face. I landed in a whole piled up bunch of mesquite. No one, I'm sure, ever since that hill was first there, ever came down it so fast.

I wasn't hurt. Except for a scratch stinging near my eye, I was all right. It didn't even bleed. All I needed was to catch my breath. I lay there in the bushes until I did. Breathing and listening for Mrs. Mertian, in case she came to the top of the hill and was yelling down at me. But I didn't hear any yelling. When I looked she wasn't there. The school bell stopped, too. All there was to hear was the thunder, now and then, far off, and the wind blowing quiet.

I got up thinking, I'd done it. After what Juby told me there was only one thing to do, and now I'd done it. Here I was, just me, Miguel, getting the sheep that were lost, all alone. And there would be no one bringing them home but me. All I had to do was to get up there, on the mesa across the river, round up the bunch and march them back to where everyone could see. It would be something worth watching, me herding the ewes and lambs that were lost back into the corral at home. My father would tell me how sorry he was about breakfast, the way he wouldn't let me go help. And I would tell my father, it was nothing, he didn't have to feel sorry.

I felt good. Looking at the mountains, and the mountains looking down at me as if to see what I was going to do next.

I hopped across the river. The easy place to cross was downstream a way, where there were more rocks to jump on. I didn't bother to go to the easy place. I could have made it even if the rocks were twice as far from each other, feeling good like I was, and all in practice from the way I'd come jumping down the hill. I only slipped into the water twice, without much water getting into my shoes at all.

To get up the cliff on the other side was not easy. It was steep in this place and wet and slippery with the rain, the stones high and smooth with nothing to grab on to except sometimes a juniper bush. And besides having the books in one hand. It would be better without the books. But I couldn't leave them around or hide them, seeing they might get wet. I made it all right, pulling and crawling my way up. Steep places and books, that wasn't too hard. Not to find a bunch of lost sheep, it wasn't.

When I got up to the top and looked, I didn't see them. I guess I did expect a little bit they'd be up there waiting for me. But they weren't. I didn't mind too much. The kind of thing I was doing had to be hard. Such a big thing couldn't be too easy. It'd be like cheating. I set out, walking to the north.

Up on the mesa, it looked empty. Like one of those pictures that Pedro draws. One straight line across the middle of the page and big zigzags off to one side which is the mountains. Then dark on top for the clouds, which he makes by smudging up all the pencil lines. And dark on the bottom for the mesa, which he makes with a special black crayon. That's all there is in the picture. And that's why it's a good picture. Because that's all there is. Except for some little bushes, juniper and chaparral and sagebrush. With nothing sticking up, only a high soapweed or a crooked looking cactus. Nothing else.

Especially, no sheep.

I walked from one rise to the next. Every three or four

steps turning all around as I walked. And when I got near to the top of each rise I had to run. Because I thought in the next ten, fifteen steps up top there, sure, I'd see them. The first few times I saw nothing, which I didn't mind too much. And the next few times, I saw nothing, too. Pretty soon I was getting ready to see them, because after an hour or so of walking and turning around and running I figured it was hard enough. Even for something big.

Besides I had a pebble in my left shoe. I felt it down there coming up the cliff. I didn't mind then, because it only made everything even harder. And that was all right with me. But now it was getting to hurt good. And I couldn't sit down and take it out. That would be like giving up.

Besides, I didn't have any time to waste. The mesa spread out, as far as you could see, with many breaks—everywhere little canyons and washes. And it was sure that on top of the next canyon, maybe, I was going to see them, those sheep. If I didn't waste time getting up there. Which I didn't. But all I saw was the same kind of nothing that I saw from the last high place, just this wide straight line stretching right across the middle.

Walking down was harder than walking up. For one thing, walking down on my left heel made the pebble bigger. It was getting to feel like a rock. And for another, walking down, you've already seen what there is to see all around, and there's nothing to look forward to until you start to walk up again. It got so I was running more than

I was walking. Running downhill because I wanted to get that part over with, and running up because I couldn't wait to get to the top. And all the time, turning around. I got pretty good at being able to turn around and keep running at the same time.

Except what good was it, getting pretty good at anything? When the only thing counted was to get one look, one quick look at those sheep.

All the turning around did was to get me so mixed up I didn't know whether I was going north, south, east or west. Not that it made any difference, I guess. The sheep weren't particular which direction you went to find them. They weren't in any direction. There were just no sheep. There was all the dark sky, and all this straight flat plain you'd ever want to see. But, no sheep.

And after a couple of hours of seeing no sheep, I would've been glad to see any sheep, even if they weren't ours. I kept trying to see sheep so hard, it was like my eyes got dry and thirsty just to see sheep. Last year, when I was looking for that Indian stone, it was a lot better. At least there were a lot of stones to look at, and that was something. But to see nothing for two, three hours, especially sheep, it gets hard on your eyes.

It was getting hard on my left foot, too, with that big rock pressing in.

And it wasn't so easy on my hands, either, on account of the books. The books weren't heavy, but when you keep that rope wrapped around your hand it can pinch.

And even if you take it off one hand and put it on the other, it don't take long before it's pinching that hand, too.

Another thing was it got to be hard breathing. Because there was no time to stop and get a good breath. There was always somewhere to go take a look, and you couldn't stop because maybe that very second the sheep were moving away out of sight, and that very second if you were up on a top you'd see them.

After so many hours of it being so hard, I figured it was hard enough by then. It was getting long past the time I ought to find our sheep. Only it didn't make any difference how I figured. They weren't there to be found. Not anywhere.

And after a while, walking, walking, every place started to look like you'd been there before. You'd see a piece of tumble weed. And you were sure it was one you saw an hour before. It didn't help to think that maybe you were just walking up and around the same hill all the time.

Then looking, looking, I thought I heard a bell. I listened hard in the wind. One of the ewes that was lost might have a bell. In the flock there are ten or a dozen sheep with bells. Each one is like the leader of a bunch. I stood still, listening. Then I heard it again, and it was for sure a bell. But it was the school bell, far away, back in Los Cordovas. It must've already become noon, and that was the bell for noontime. Soon the ringing far away stopped. And there was nothing to listen to again, except the quiet wind.

It was never the same, after I heard that bell. It made

me feel hungry. Because the bell meant going home to eat. And feeling hungry, I got to feel not so good in the other parts of me. Like lonely. At the beginning being alone was the best part of it, going off by myself to bring home the sheep. But now it was getting to look like I wasn't bringing home any sheep. And that made a lot of difference about being alone, while everybody else was back there going home to eat. The only way I could go home was to find them. It wasn't only so I could bring the sheep back. I had to find them so I could go back, too.

From then on, I got very busy. I didn't stop to walk any more. I ran. Everywhere I went I kept up running, and I did most of my breathing going downhill when I didn't have to try so hard to keep running. There was hardly any breath left over to keep looking with. And that was the hardest part of all, the looking. Because there was never anything to see.

And after a long while, I heard the bell again. School was out for the day.

It was hard to figure out what to do next.

I could leave home. That's about all that was left. I couldn't go back without the sheep. Not after what my father said at breakfast, and especially not after the way he looked. And it was clear enough that in all this whole empty place I was never going to find them, those sheep. I could just as well stop, that's all. I could take some time and do a lot of breathing. I could bury my books under a bush. I could sit down and take off my shoe and get rid of that rock with all the sharp edges on it. Then I could go some-where until I saw a lot of sheep and sit down and look at them, till I got enough again of looking at sheep. And then I could decide where I was leaving home to go to.

Maybe even to the Sangre de Cristo Mountains. On my own, by myself.

But when I looked at the mountains, I knew that was no good. It was impossible. There was only one way to go up into the Mountains of the Sangre de Cristo. And that was to make everyone see you were ready, and then you would go.

Indeed, in order that I should go this way, that's why I was looking for the sheep right now. And if I gave up looking for the sheep, then the idea of going up into the Mountains, I had to give that up, too. I guess if you are going to leave home you just left home, that's all, every-thing.

Except, it wasn't up to me anymore. It wasn't a question that I should give up looking for the sheep.

It was just no use.

I could keep running from the top of one rise up to the next, looking, looking with my eyes getting drier and drier, without any breath, and the bones in my hands like they were cracking, and the heel of my left foot like it was getting torn away, listening to nothing but the wind—I could keep on doing that forever. It wasn't a question of me giving up, it was a question that just everything had given up, me and everything.

So I sat down. I took a deep breath. And I started to untie the laces from my left shoe. And then—what do you think?

I smelled them.

CHAPTER 7

IT IS not hard to know that what you're smelling is sheep. If only there are some sheep around to smell. They smell a little sweet and a little old, like coffee that's left over in a cup on the table with maybe used up cigarettes in it. That's sort of what they smell like.

So when there was this smell, I looked around. I found out from which direction was the wind. And in that direction I went to the top of the next rise, a dozen steps. And no farther away than you could throw a rock, there they were coming up the hill toward me, about fifteen ewes and their lambs, ambling along, having a good time eating, just taking a walk like there was no trouble anywhere in all the world.

"Wahoo!" I took off. Around my head in a big circle I swung my books. Like it was a rope, and I was going to throw a loop on all fifteen at once. "Wahoo!" I took off down that hill as if I were a whole tribe of Indians and the sheep was somebody's chuck wagon that was going to get raided. "Wahoo!"

The sheep looked up, a little like they were a bunch of ladies in church and they were interested to see who was coming through the door.

I showed them who was coming through the door. Before they knew what was happening they were moving. *Whoosh*—I let my books swing out, and I hit one right in the rump. *Whish*—I kicked another one with my foot that had the rock, so that it hurt me more, I think, than the sheep. I picked up a stone and—*wango*—I let a third one have it in the rear. I got them running right in the opposite direction than they were going.

I kept them going at a gallop. Running first to the one side, then to the other, swinging the books around my head all the time. Yelling and hollering so they wouldn't even dare slow down. They looked scared, but I didn't care. I had waited too long for this. And now I wanted them to know that I was here. I ran them down the hill fast enough to be a stampede. And whichever one ran last, he was the unlucky one. There were a lot of rocks around, and I throw rocks good.

At the bottom of the hill I quieted down. Why was I acting like I was so mad? I had no reason to be mad at the sheep. It wasn't as if they started out to get me in trouble. Indeed, because of them, here I was doing a great thing. I was finding them and bringing them home. If they didn't take it into their heads to go out and get lost, I never would have this big chance.

I quieted down. I stopped and I breathed. The air was good. After the rain it was clean and it smelled sweet, like a vanilla soda in Schaeffer's Drugstore in Taos before you start to drink it with the straw. I took in the air with deep breaths. I sat down and took off my shoe. I found the rock down near the heel. But my goodness, it wasn't any kind of rock at all. Just a little bit of a chip off a stone. In my foot it felt like a boulder. But in my hand it didn't look like anything at all.

I was quieted down. We started off. It was going to be a long drive home. I didn't mind. There were so many good things to think about. What my father would say to me and my grandfather.

It is no great trouble to drive a small bunch of sheep. You just walk behind them, and if one begins to separate you start in the same direction that it starts and that makes it turn back and bunch up again. It was very little work. So there was much time to think what my uncles would say, and my big brothers. And how Pedro would watch me.

There was much time to look around. At the mountains, not so dark now and not so mad. There was much to see, walking along thinking, breathing, and looking around. How the clouds now were taking on new shapes, the dark ones separating and new big white ones coming up. And on the mesa everything looked fine. I saw flowers. Before when I was looking there were no flowers. Now, there they were. The little pink ones of the peyote plants. And there were flowers on the hedgehog cactus, too, kind of pinkish purple some, and others a real red.

I remembered Gabriel's song about the little red flower. And walking along, thinking, breathing, looking around, I began to sing the song. Only the first words over and over again because I didn't remember the rest, which made no difference, because who was listening anyway? It was just I wanted something to sing.

After a little while I had something else to do. One of the lambs lay down. Whether it was tired or why, I don't know. I picked it up, the lamb under my arm, and in the other hand the rope with my books. It was not so bad. Even the rope didn't pinch anymore. And when the lamb got heavy under one arm, I put it under the other.

The number of the lamb was 119. I remembered the morning I put the number on him. That day was one of the best days as far as how many lambs came. When it started we were only using two numbers, around 83 or 84.

Then I had to use three irons when we got to a hundred. Before the day was over we were already making numbers in the one-twenties.

Some of the other numbers in the bunch I remembered too. Like 251, and 170 and 582. They were like friends these numbers, that is the ewes with these numbers and the lambs. They were my friends. And I was their pas*tor*. I was the one who put numbers on them. And I was the one who brought them home, now, from being lost.

I felt better, now, than in a long time.

Even when I had to pick up this second lamb which was straggling behind, I still felt good. It was harder this way because now I couldn't use one arm after the other when the lambs got heavy, and there were the books I had to carry in addition. By now though we were coming down the dry wash that led to the river. There was not much further to go.

They were a good bunch of sheep, all of them. When I brought them to the place in the river that was not so deep, they waded right across without any trouble. As for me myself, I almost fell in but all the way this time. I was balancing myself all right on the rocks going across when 119 started to wriggle like it wanted to shake itself apart. But I held on, and I kept my balance and didn't fall in. I wouldn't have minded, anyway, if I had. If I came to the house with all my clothes wet, that would make what I did look as if it was even harder than it was.

Blasito was the first one to see me.

He was walking across the top of the hill near the corral when I came around the bend from the river.

"Hey, Mickey," he yelled, "where you been? What's those sheep you got?"

"Yours," I shouted back.

"Mine? What do you mean mine? The lost ones?"

"That's what," I yelled. "The lost ones!"

"No! No fooling?" He turned away from me. "Ai Grandpa. Padre de Chavez. Mira! Miguel's here, with the bunch that was lost!" He looked back to where I was coming up the hill. "Bravo, Miguelito! Where'd you find them? How did it happen?"

"I'll tell you." I needed my breath to get up the hill with those two lambs under my arms. "Wait'll I get there."

The two of them were waiting for me, Blasito and my grandfather. Grandpa took one of the lambs from my arms. I let the other one down. Blasito shooed the bunch into the corral. And all three of us talked at once.

"Where did you find them?" asked Blasito.

"How did this happen?" said Grandfather.

"I'll tell it to you all," I said, "from the beginning. On the way to school this morning I started to think."

Blasito interrupted. "Can't you tell us where you found them?"

"But that's what I'm trying to do. It started on the way to school."

"Miguel," my grandfather wouldn't let me talk. "That part you can tell us later. Where were they, the sheep?"

"Well, I'll tell you that first, then. I found them on the way to Arroyo Hondo, about twenty or thirty miles from here. But the way it started—"

"How many miles?" My grandfather looked at me with a smile.

"Oh many miles, many, many. What happened was—"

"How come you went north?" asked Blas. "All morning we've been riding toward the Arroyo del Alamo. In just the other way."

"First comes the way I went down the hill," I tried to explain. "With world record jumps."

"Why is it that you don't want to answer your big brother Blas?" asked Grandpa. "How did you know where to look?"

"But why can't I tell it the way it happened? There was much trouble and it's very interesting."

"Later," said Grandpa. "Now, how did you know?"

"Well, I figured it out, and then I kept my ears open to hear things."

"What things?" said Blasito.

"Things people say?"

"Like who?"

"Like Juby."

"He told you?"

"Look," I said to Blasito. "If I can't tell you in my own way, then what's the use? The kind of questions you ask, it makes it all sound like nothing. If I have to tell it this way, just to answer a few little questions, then what's the use my going out and finding the sheep anyway?"

"Use?" Blasito started to laugh. He banged me on the back. "It's a great thing, finding those sheep. I mean it, Miguel. You did fine!"

"What did you say?"

"I said great, fine!"

Grandfather took me by the hand and shook it like when two men shake hands.

"It's the truth," he said. "This that you have done, it was good."

"What?" I asked my Grandfather.

"It was good."

"Better than the rest of us could do," said Blasito.

"What?" I asked Blasito.

"Better than the rest of us!" Blasito shouted so I would hear.

Grandpa still held my hand, and he shook it again. "You brought them in all right, Miguel. Like a real pastor."

"What?" I asked my grandfather. I wanted to hear everything twice.

"A real pastor," Grandpa said again, and we all looked at each other and smiled.

"Anything else?" I asked.

Before anyone could answer, there was a great shout from the house. "Miguel!" It was my father. It was a shout that sounded like thunder. "Miguel, get over here!"

He stood, he and my mother both, they stood in front of the house. And with them was Mrs. Mertian, my school-teacher. They stood with Mrs. Mertian who had come from the school in Los Cordovas, and they talked to-gether.

My father looked around at us once again. "Miguel!"

Grandpa nodded to me that I should go to my father. "Take off," said Blasito. "You'd better get going."

I went. What else? It was too bad, real bad, my teacher should talk to my father before I even got a chance. I knew now that the things I was thinking about on the way home, of what my father would say to me, I knew that these were probably not the things he was going to say to me now. I walked to the house where they stood, and Mrs. Mertian smiled at my mother and they shook hands, then she smiled at my father and shook hands with him. Then everybody smiled at each other and she left. But when they turned to watch me coming up the path, my father and mother, nobody smiled.

"Where'd you go?" said my father.

"Up there to the Arroyo Hondo. Many miles."

"What's in Arroyo Hondo?"

I knew my father didn't want to know what's in Arroyo Hondo. He knew as well as I. Just a grocery store and some houses. If I told him that then everything would get all mixed up the way it did.

"It was not for what's in Arroyo Hondo. It's that I went after the sheep that were lost."

98

"This morning at breakfast, didn't we talk about the lost sheep?"

"Yes." I knew what he meant. "And you told me to go to school. And I did, I went to school."

"That is true. But it is only one small piece of what is true. The rest is, you didn't go in."

"Because of Juby. He is my oldest friend."

"And why is it, Miguel, that you will obey your oldest friend? But your parents, who are friends to you even older than your oldest friend, what they say means nothing."

"But Juby told me where were the missing sheep. So I went. I got them. I brought them home."

This is not the way I wanted to tell it at all. It was worse than with Blasito and Grandpa. It didn't sound hard this way, or like a big thing. It was like going down to the spring for a pail of water, no more. But what else was there to do? If things kept up like they were, it could get bad.

"You brought what home?"

"The missing sheep. They are in the corral."

My father and mother looked. Blasito and my grandfather, who were watching us, they pointed out the bunch in the corral.

"Well!" My father, at least, he didn't sound so mad anymore when he looked back to me.

"That's why I didn't go to school."

"Well," my father put his hands in his back pockets and looked down at me. "That's different. But not so different

99

to make too much difference, Miguel. Sheep are important. Sure! But you, too, that you go to school is important. Even more important. Always there has to be something done with the sheep. And if every time something had to be done, you stayed away from school, my goodness, you'd grow up to be a burro. And you tell me, do we need a burro around this place?"

"No. Only mules and horses."

"And even more, what we need is young men who are educated, who have learned to know what is the difference between what is right and what is wrong. Do you understand?"

"I understand. And I promise. I will never miss my school again."

"Good, now get into the house. Mrs. Mertian brought the lessons from today. So go in and do them and write your homework for tomorrow."

My mother took me by the back of the head to go into the house with me. And then my father did a wonderful thing. He gave me one good spank. And when I looked around up at him, he was smiling.

"It would not be true," he told me, "if I didn't say also I am glad to have the sheep back. How you did it was wrong. But for what you did, I want to thank you."

And then he went off to go to Blas and Grandpa where they were working on the tractor. My mother took me with her into the house.

"Come, Miquito. That's enough for today. Good and bad, you've done enough."

But it wasn't enough. I wanted to say "What?" to my father, so he would say it, and I would hear it again how he thanked me. This was as much as I could hope. To have my father actually thank me the way he did, for something real, not for like just passing the bread across the table. But doing for the flock what no one else had been able to do! And the way his voice sounded when he said it. Real serious, as if he were making a plan with Ernie Gutierrez, who is the county agent.

It wasn't enough. At a time like this something more had to happen. As soon as my mother went into the kitchen, I ran back out again. Out to where my father was with Blasito and Grandpa, working on the tractor.

I don't know what was wrong with the tractor. It was coughing and rattling and starting up and stopping, the way tractors do sometimes. I was not so lucky. By the time I got out to the barnyard it started up with a great roar. And the heads of all three of them, my father, brother, and Grandpa, were buried inside the machine where they were twisting the screws around in there. I shouted. But in such a great roar they didn't hear me. So I had to wait until someone looked up.

My father was the first to notice me. I couldn't hear him but from the way he looked I knew he was saying, what was I doing out there?

I had to shout as loud as I could. "First I have to tell you about when you said 'Thank you,' back there."

"Yes," he had to yell down at me, "what do you want to tell me?"

"You're welcome."

"Okay," he smiled and started to turn back to the tractor. "Now get back to your lessons."

"Something else!" I yelled. The noise got even bigger. It was hard to shout so loud.

"What?"

"I got to explain about school."

"Blasito," yelled my father. "Throttle her down. Less gas!"

"I can't." Blasito raised his hands, and he yelled something about the carburetor and the intake and the manifold and I don't know what.

"Well, anyway," my father shouted at me, "what is it?"

If it was up to me to arrange how things should be at this moment, when I had to say what I must say, it would not be like this. If it was up to me, my father and I would be alone in some quiet place like the big church that we sometimes go to in Ranchos, just he and me alone in our best clothes that we wear on Easter. It would be very quiet when I told him after so many years what I had to tell him, so that he could listen real serious the way he was when he said "Thank you."

Now, it was like it must be with a war going on, with the banging and exploding and the roar.

But it was too late, now, not to go ahead. Now, when everything was just right, I couldn't say, "Well, nothing," and walk away. No matter what, it had to be now. So I took a deep, deep breath and I shouted, my hands to my mouth.

"School. Soon it will be all over. Vacation time."

"Yes?"

"Then—I can help? With the flock? Every day?"

"Sure!"

This was good. This was fine. Now there was just one more question to ask. Only one more minute to get over with.

"Then. When I don't have to go to school? When I can help every day? Then. I can go to the mountains? With the others? For summer pasture? Yes?"

"What?" yelled my father.

"I can go to the mountains? Yes?"

My father looked down at me, he didn't answer. And Grandfather looked. And Blasito, too. And even the engine of the tractor, it stopped. It was quiet.

"No!" It was like a bugle busting out. My father yelled as if the engine was still making a racket. I must've jumped, the way he put his hand on my shoulder to keep me steady.

"I'm sorry," said my father. "I've been yelling so much."

"I know," I said. "The noise."

"But about going with the flock, for the pasture this summer, it cannot be arranged. Not this year." He nodded off to where my brother Gabriel was working on the hay

103

pile. "Gabriel will go, as in the years past. That's part of his work. For you, it's not yet time."

"Not yet time," I said.

We all of us just stood there looking at each other. Then my father, instead of saying something, he shook his head. I looked at my grandfather. And he, too, shook his head. I looked at Blasito. Blasito looked away from me down into the engine again and started making noises with a wrench.

"Miguel," I turned back to my father. "I have not yet finished," he told me. "This summer, you too will have an important job. Instead of the girls, it will be you who will take care of him."

He pointed with his head, and when I turned to look what he was pointing at it was Jimmy, the orphan, by himself in one corner of the corral.

"You will take care of the orphan."

I turned back. "The orphan."

Then we stood around looking at each other for a little while longer. Except Blas, who was busy with the motor, he didn't look up.

After a while my father said, "Okay?"

And I said, "Yes, Padre." I just stood. I didn't know what else to do.

Then the motor started again, because of Blas fiddling with it I guess, and they all looked back at the motor. After I watched them working for a while, I went away.

I walked to the corral and climbed through the fence and went through the sheep looking at the numbers here and

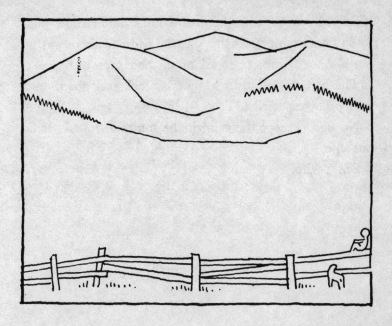

there, and then Jimmy came running up. So I stopped and
gave him a few pats on the head, and we both looked back
to where the men were working. They had the engine
going fine by now, the three of them.

I patted Jimmy some more. He, without his number, the
orphan I was to take care of here on the farm all summer.
I patted him because there was nothing else to do. My
father said no. Even my grandfather, he who had called me
a real pas*tor*, he too said no. What worse could there be?
I finished patting Jimmy and walked over to the fence on
the far side of the corral. I climbed up and sat down on
the fence, looking away from the farm.

It was a nice day, it certainly did turn out nice. And they

105

looked nice in the sun, the mountains. I didn't know what to do because, now, all this was the end and there was no one else to ask, no one to ask or anymore even to hope.

The Sangre de Cristo Mountains look real good, on a sunny day, especially.

No one—except there might be someone to ask, some one else.

San Ysidro.

CHAPTER 8

SAN YSIDRO is a saint that I know.

There are many saints, many many, about whom I don't know anything. There are some saints even whose name I can't remember. But San Ysidro is a saint that I know very well for a long time.

One thing about San Ysidro is that he's a saint for all the farmers everywhere, that is, all the farmers in the world. When a farmer has to have something very important, like good crops, or rain, or to fix up a cow that is bad with colic, and there is no one else to ask, San Ysidro is there to be asked.

But the other thing about San Ysidro is that he's special for us. He is the patron saint of our village of Los Cordovas. That means, in addition to taking care of all the farmers everywhere and listening to what they ask and deciding whether it's good or no good and arranging the way it should be for them, besides all that he keeps an eye out special for Los Cordovas.

He has done fine for Los Cordovas. In our village we have never had an earthquake so that the ground cracks open, or any volcanos so that fire comes out of the hills, or any big floods that cover up all the houses, or any big wars or anything that was too bad. For as long as I can remember, there have been no complaints about how San Ysidro has handled things for our village.

Most Sundays it is not San Ysidro to whom we pray. On every Sunday except one we go to church and pray regular about all the regular things we have to be, like good, for instance. But one Sunday, always around the middle of May, we go and pray to San Ysidro and ask him for the special things that we ourselves most want. This year San Ysidro Day was on May fifteenth.

It begins at Vespers. That's when the sun goes down. And this year Vespers was held at our new chapel, not yet finished, that is on the other side of Los Cordovas from us on the road to Ranchos. The chapel is being built by my father and our neighbors. For a year or longer they've

108

been getting together every once in a while and making bricks of adobe and building the walls. Until now everything is finished except the roof and the doors and windows and what goes inside. All that is needed to finish, from what I hear, is more time for the men to work and also some money.

So this year Vespers was outside. My mother and the other ladies fixed up the altar nice, with lace they had and branches with leaves on and flowers. And everyone brought chairs, besides the ones they got from the big church in Ranchos. It looked nice. When the Father, who came from the church in Ranchos, got behind the altar, and the altar boys to one side with these big white collars, and the nuns who were for the choir, and in the sky gold and shadows with red from the way the sun was setting, it looked real nice. On the walls of what was going to be the chapel, behind the altar, were put *luminarias*. These are like lanterns that you make by putting sand in a paper bag and a candle in the sand.

When you light them up and set them on your roof it means a big holiday, for instance Christmas. Or San Ysidro Day. And the way everything looked this San Ysidro Day I'd just as soon always go to church outside.

This year we had a new San Ysidro, that is to say a new statue of him that was on the altar. It was carved from wood by George Perez who lives up there in Truchas—or maybe it's Trampas—anyway, up there in the hills which is just at the beginning of the Sangre de Cristo. The pictures

109

of San Ysidro are all the same. First there is the saint, himself. And then always a plow with oxen. And behind is the angel who you can always tell because she is the one with the wings. Our new San Ysidro, also, was like this.

But as soon as I saw him, I knew I was lucky. When I say I knew, I mean there was this feeling I had, that he and I, we'd get along good. While everyone was praying along with the choir and the altar boys, I studied the new San Ysidro very close. He looked all right, like someone you could talk to and not get mixed up. Besides he came from Truchas, or maybe Trampas, but anyway from up there, from where they started, at least, the mountains. When I asked him, one thing was he'd know what I was talking about and why it was so important.

I never did get to ask him at Vespers. What happened is, I studied him so close without thinking the way the prayers were going that, when I did take notice and found how far along everyone else had got, it was like the last half of the ninth inning and no time left. I couldn't ask in any fast way. It had to be just right. This time it was not like having tractors around and people yelling, a lot of noise. There was only San Ysidro to talk to, quiet. There was only this last, this very last chance. And it had to be just right.

After Vespers, the way it is on San Ysidro Day, a lot of us took, from where they were piled up, a torch. These are branches tied tight together and you stick them in the bonfires that are started in the dark. Then everyone got in a long line, those of us with torches holding them up over our head. And we all went walking down the road to Mrs. Esposito's house, the Father and the altar boys and the choir up front, singing hymns.

I had a torch. And by then, after I decided I wouldn't do my asking until after Mass the next morning, I followed the hymns along with everyone else. It was good, singing hymns. Not that I knew what any of them meant. They were all in Latin. But they sounded important. More important, for instance, than "On Top Of Old Smoky" which everyone can understand and is all right for every day. But in a time like this, when everything meant a lot, I'd just as soon have a hymn to sing.

The next day everyone comes to Mass in their best clothes. At Vespers some don't have the time to change before they must go from plowing or their sheep or whatever it is they happened to be doing. But on the morning of San Ysidro Day they all look like they were from one of those books my mother gets every month that has pictures of ladies and men in their best clothes and also pictures of the kind of things to eat that you never see anywhere else. I dressed up, too, in a new blue shirt that was just the same color as my dungarees, the pair I have with no holes in it or patches.

After Mass comes the big part of San Ysidro Day. We make what is called a Procession, a parade, like. We all walk up to where the road forks off. Then out into the fields. We kneel down. Mrs. Esposito carries San Ysidro

111

from the altar. She stands holding it now in front of the Father. And while we pray, he blesses all the fields of our valley, waving his hand to the north, then to the south, then the east, then west.

He blesses in Latin. But I know, because I have been told, what it means. It is to make the earth which we work healthy and good. So that, all in our valley, they should have a fine harvest. And everyone a good year, generally. He asks San Ysidro to please arrange matters in this way.

This is the most important part of all the praying, when the fields are blessed. For at the same time that the Father is waving his hand first in one direction then the other, each one prays for himself what is in his heart. My father, I figured he would pray for the alfalfa field of thirteen acres that we have on the other side of the river, on account of it didn't do so good last year. And I guess the rest in my family had something to pray for, too. Except Pedro, for whom everything was enough. And Faustina, who didn't understand what it was all about anyway.

Since the night before when I didn't get a chance to say my wish at Vespers, I was waiting for this time. Only now that it was here, I wasn't ready. It is not easy to make a prayer that is a wish as important as this one. Ordinarily, I'm a pretty good prayer. I can do an "Our Father who Art In Heaven" as fast as anybody else. Without skipping words, I can beat even my big sisters. But this wish wasn't like doing an "Our Father." I had to make up the words for this one myself.

112

And not only words. To say a wish like this one I think maybe you have to say it with something more than just plain words. The plain kind of words are good for the plain, regular kind of things. Like when Uncle Eli asks me what was the next number I would tell him "One eighty-seven" or whatever the number is. Or if Pedro says, "When's dinner?" I would say, "Now," or "Soon." For such things, there are words that are easy to understand.

But for anything more important, words get mixed up. They get to be like "okeydokee" or "babaloo," Faustina's words that just mean nothing at all. Sometimes when I talk to my father or to my mother or to anyone at all about something that's really important, I could just as well say "Babaloo, babaloo, babaloo" for all anyone understands. And if that's the way it was with my father and mother, how much harder to find the right way of talking to someone you don't know half so good, like San Ysidro, about something that was twice as important as anything you ever had to talk about. What I had to find was some new way, the right way to talk. Otherwise it would be like going to High Mass with the Father standing up there in front, and the altar boys on one side and the nuns making a choir on the other, and me standing in the middle singing "On Top Of Old Smoky."

So there I was, kneeling out there in the fields along with everyone else, all of us spread out around Mrs. Esposito who was holding San Ysidro, and the Father waving his hand to the north and south and so forth, and me trying

114

to study out a whole new way to make my wish before it was too late.

The way I studied was by looking at San Ysidro as hard as I could, in order I should get to know him as good as I could in so short a time—looking hard at every little crack in his face, at each feather in the wings of the angel. There were six feathers on each side. And at the same time I held my hands together as tight as I could, until my knuckles began to hurt. And with my knees I pressed into the ground as heavy as I could, pressing so hard I felt almost as if I was going to sink in.

I tried with my insides, too. Last winter my friend Juby had a way of talking without moving his lips. He used to say "Look out—you're gonna get hit!" and you had to look real close before you saw that it was him saying it. He used a different kind of voice, and it seemed to be coming, the voice, almost from somewhere else than Juby. Talking like this was not hard, Juby explained to me, it was done with the stomach, by working it around with a twist, and he tried to show me how. But I only got started learning when the big storm we had came, and then we forgot everything because there was so much to do with the snow.

I tried it now, because it was certainly a new way of talking and might be just right for a time like this. Only "Look out—you're going to get hit!" had nothing to do with what I wanted to say, and I was having a hard time getting my stomach worked around to say anything else. So that before you know it with looking so hard, and my hands clasped so tight, and my knees pressing so heavy, and my stomach all twisted, I felt funny. Like dizzy.

I closed my eyes and I prayed. I prayed to God like he should introduce me to San Ysidro and say, "I want you to meet a friend of mine, by the name Miguel. See what you can do for him."

But I hadn't made the wish to San Ysidro himself yet when I opened my eyes and there was everybody crossing themselves and saying "Amen" and one or two getting up from kneeling. The prayers were coming to an end. It had to be said, the wish, whichever way it could. Right now!

"San Ysidro," I closed my eyes. "Dear sir. If you think it's a good idea, please arrange it I should go up into the mountains, the Sangre de Cristo. I know it's a hard thing to do, but whichever way you do it, no matter how, is all right with me, Miguel. Thanks."

And at that moment, I felt a tap on my shoulder.

All dressed up and with a tie the way he was on special days, there was my father. "That's enough, Miguelito," he said. "Services are finished."

"Finished," I said. And when I let go of everything, my hands and knees and eyes and stomach, I almost fell over.

I didn't want to get up. It was finished. I'd said it. And it was no good. No good. It was just like saying to Pedro that dinner would be soon. What I said was nothing special. It would never work. I was sure of it, the wish would never work. It was finished.

My father put down his hand. When I took it, he pulled

116

me to my feet. It was just as well he helped me, now that it was all over. I could never have got up by myself.

After the services comes a fiesta. This is almost as important a part of San Ysidro Day as the blessing of the fields. And for anyone that is hungry, who wants something to eat, I guess it is even more important. There is a lot to eat. At the fiesta I can never understand how come you hear so much laughing and talking and joking and singing. The way there is so much to eat, and the way it all gets eaten up, you'd think that what you'd hear at a fiesta is nothing but a lot of people standing around chewing. But even though much gets eaten, there is a lot of other noise besides.

This year the fiesta was held on our place, under the big cottonwood tree near the river where Gabriel plans to build himself an adobe house. The making of the food started very early, almost in the middle of the night. Juan Moreno, who comes from El Prado, and Al Summers were in charge of the cooking. Two days before, they dug a pit under the cottonwood tree, maybe six feet long and six feet deep and three feet wide. On the day before they brought down from the hills a truck load of special wood, *piñon* and oak. And at four in the morning, before it was light, on San Ysidro Day they started the fire.

The reason they get started so early is that cooking for a fiesta is not like cooking on a kitchen stove. Before anything, you've got to burn up all the wood until the pit is

117

filled with red hot coals that are on fire. Then on top of the pit you put an old spring from a bed, and on top of this you cook the meat. They do it this way because this is called a barbecue, and you can't have a fiesta without a barbecue. The food is supposed to be ready when the services end, which is another reason they get started so early. But it never is. And everybody stands around smelling how good dinner is going to be and drinking—some wine, some beer, and bottles of soda for the kids—and making fun of the cooks, saying that everything they are doing is all wrong and if anyone is hungry it would be better they go into town and have a sandwich at Schaeffer's Drugstore.

I didn't drink anything. I wasn't very thirsty. I sat on a rock and watched Mr. Moreno and Mr. Summers cook. It's interesting because it looks like they are making dinner for a giant. They use a pitchfork to turn the meat over, and instead of a spoon they use a shovel, and big buckets instead of pots. When Mr. Moreno says to Mr. Summers, "I think maybe now it needs just a little bit more sauce," Mr. Summers throws over the meat one whole big bucket of sauce, tossing it like he was washing down a horse.

People come to the fiesta not only from Los Cordovas but from all around, more than come to the church. This is bad, says my grandfather, that they should want to eat more than to pray. Maybe so, but I think if you're hungry you might as well go ahead and eat if there's food around all cooked and ready. It's fine to pray except you never know what's going to be. But if you are hungry and you have a plate of food, at least you know soon you won't be hungry anymore.

For myself, I wasn't hungry. I watched how the others ate. Everyone stood in a long line, one behind the other, without pushing, each one holding a plate; and they went by this long table behind which stood my mother and my sisters and other ladies from the church. On each plate as it went by the ladies put food from pots that were on the table, *frijoles*, which is cooked beans, and chili sauce and *ensalada de col y cebolla*, which is like cole slaw, and peaches from cans and biscuits.

At the next table stands Mr. Moreno behind big chunks of meat, which is now all roasted and steaming and sending out smells that go everywhere like a song you listen to with your nose, not your ears. The way he stood, with a big fork in one hand and a long knife in the other, Mr. Moreno looked like a man with a bull fiddle I once saw in a band in Taos, standing up behind the meat and slicing. Everyone stood around watching the juice run out and pointing out which pieces they wanted on their plate, red meat or maybe a little burnt or with a bone. And over it all Mr. Summers ladled out barbecue sauce from this pot as big, almost, as a bath tub.

To drink there was everything there was before, like beer, and now coffee, too. And cake. There were more different kinds because each lady in the church baked her special kind. And each one kept her eye out to see that everyone else took a piece. None of them saw me though, where I was.

By the time you got away from the tables you had your arms full. Then each one went and sat around under the trees and along the river, eating and telling each other jokes. I didn't go down from my rock to where they were because I couldn't think of any jokes.

After awhile, when everybody was beginning to have enough to eat, there was dancing. Mr. Medina, who teaches in the high school in Taos, came with his fiddle, a regular-sized one. Mr. Medina is an expert at fiddle playing, and I've never seen him break even one string. Then there was Dick Montoya with one guitar, and my big brother Blasito who brought out his guitar from the house, and that made two. Once they started playing, the three of them the same song together, most everybody took a chance at dancing.

I didn't dance. First because I don't know how to very good, not the kind of dancing you do at a fiesta. Juby and I and some of the others, we do a kind of Indian dance that has to have special music which you play by hitting sticks on a fence and yelling. But you don't dance that way when you have a fiddle and two guitars, and even if you did, I don't think I would have danced anyway. I didn't feel like dancing. I felt more like watching.

After a while it just got down to a bunch from the high school dancing, and then everyone watched. This bunch

they always dance together. The girls have all sewed for themselves the same kind of dress, and the boys all wear white shirts, and they go and dance for the high school like the baseball team goes and plays ball against some other school. Only they don't dance against anybody or keep score, it's just to go and show off how good they are, which is pretty good, everyone says. Once they even went to St. Louis, a city far away from here, just to dance.

My sister Tomasita is part of this dancing bunch and so is my brother, Gabriel, and they dance about as good as anybody. I got off this rock I was on to go down with all the others and have a closer look. It was interesting to watch Tomasita because she looked so fine, the way her skirts swung out straight like a wheel whenever she turned around. But it was not so interesting to watch Gabriel.

This was not because he was no good as a dancer. He was a very good dancer. He could turn around and around without getting dizzy, and he jiggled his feet without ever tripping or falling over. And when he clapped his hands it was just exactly right with the music, sometimes even beating the others by clapping first. He danced good because he was Gabriel and everything he did was good, whether it was being a president, or playing basketball or working as a shepherd and going to the mountains.

That was the reason why it wasn't so interesting to watch anymore. Because if you had to be so good as Gabriel, then what chance could there be? Even if I had made my wish to San Ysidro all right, even perfect, it was too much to ask. To make me so good as Gabriel! Even for a first-class saint like San Ysidro it wasn't possible.

And the truth is, I didn't make the wish all right or even good.

So, not wanting to watch anymore, I thought I might as well go back to the house. And I did.

When I walked across the barnyard, Jimmy showed up. The orphan. He followed me because he was hungry and I was the one nowadays who fed him. If there was anyone I didn't want to see right then it was Jimmy. He reminded me, in another way, how what happened was the last chance and that now it was gone. And how it was going to be this

122

summer, me taking care of him, both of us hanging around the farm.

When I heard that baa of his behind me I just swung around and let go with a kick. The kick didn't land; I didn't mean that it should. All I wanted to do was scare him so he should stop following me around, reminding me.

But it didn't do any good because when I opened the gate he was still after me, giving a couple of baas. I turned, and the way Jimmy looked was like he was mad with me for trying to kick him and unhappy in general. To tell you the truth, it was the first thing since that morning which made me feel a little good, seeing Jimmy unhappy. At least he wasn't making jokes and laughing and eating and dancing like everything in the whole world was just fine. The way some people act you'd think there was no reason ever to feel unhappy.

So I went back and tried to make him feel better. I knelt down and took his head in the crook of my arm and gave it a couple of pats. But it didn't make any difference. He kept on being as sad as before, watching a bunch of sheep on the other side of the fence like that's where he wanted to be. I kept on patting him anyway, even though it didn't make any difference, watching the Sangre de Cristo Mountains. It was quiet except for that fiddle and guitar music far off on the other side of the river.

No matter how Jimmy felt, after being sad for a few minutes and quiet, with no one around having a good time, I began to feel a little better. It wasn't as if anything had changed. Nothing could change. It was finished. Except for like one of these miracles. Where the fellow that was ate up got out of this big fish, this whale. Or the other fellow that gave one blow on a bugle and all the walls fell down. Miracles like that happen. But not in our neighborhood. Not recently anyway. It wasn't much to hope for.

But, no matter what, I did feel better.

Not Jimmy, though.

So I went into the house and got the empty beer bottle and filled it with milk. I put the nipple on it and went out and fed him. That made him feel better, a lot better, by then he felt much better than me.

CHAPTER 9

"I THINK tomorrow we start bringing the bunches together. They'll be here the beginning of next week, the shearers, and it's time we collected the whole flock on our place. What do you think?"

It was my father who was talking this way, during the first days in June right after the school closed for the year. It was nothing so surprising, what he said. The surprise was that he said it to me, at least that's the way it looked.

"You mean me?" I asked.

We were walking back from the alfalfa field, the one

across the river, where we had been irrigating and fixing fences. My father, Blasito, and Gabriel and me.

"Yes," said my father, "you."

Why, with the others around, should he ask me? "I don't know," I answered truthfully, "what to think."

"Why not?"

"It's just I ain't been thinking."

"About nothing?"

"Only about supper," I told him. "About what there could be for supper."

"That's for Mama and the girls to figure out. Their worry. What we got to worry about is the flock."

This was true, so I said, "Well, if you let me worry about it for a little while then maybe I can tell you what I do think."

"Take your time," said my father. "No rush."

I worried about it all the way back to the house. If we brought the whole flock on the place too soon, then there wouldn't be enough pasture for all to eat until the shearing was done. If we didn't collect the flock, and the shearers came a day or so before expected, as sometimes they do, then there would be a great rush and not enough men to be both in the shearing sheds and out herding the sheep in, and we'd hold up the shearers and it would be bad. I didn't know how to figure too good how much pasture was needed or for how many days there was enough, or what was the latest news about where the shearers were working in the valley, but I thought about it as hard as I could. By the time we got to the house, I thought I'd take a chance.

"Now," I told my father, "I know what I think."

"What?"

"It's okay."

"To start bringing them in tomorrow?"

"Yes."

"Fine, I think so too," said my father. "That's what we'll do."

This happened the first day after school stopped. And two days later something else.

We were out fixing a pen around the shearing sheds, a place we could fill up with sheep waiting to be clipped, right close to the shearers so they could just reach out and get one they could grab. This time besides my father and me there was Uncle Bonifacio and Gabriel.

This time my father said to me, "Remember that kind of cutting-out gate they had over at the Millers'?"

I looked around to make sure he wasn't talking to the others. "Me? Remember?"

"Over at the ranch of Pete Miller, when we went last April? They had a swinging gate, a little door, rigged up right next to the shearing pens?"

"Oh," I remembered. "Mr. Miller's. That gate." It was good, too. Right next to their shearing pen they built like an alley out of fence siding, an alley about twenty feet long and just wide enough for one sheep to pass. At the end of

127

this alley, this chute, there were two openings—one into a corral, and the other into the shearing pen. Between the two openings they had only one gate, this swinging gate. Then all you had to do was to drive the bunch through the chute, and, if you wanted one sheep to go into the corral, you swung the door around to close off the pen. If you wanted the next sheep to go into the pen, you swung the door around to close off the corral. This way you could cut out whatever sheep you wanted and send them where you wanted them to go, just by driving them through the chute and swinging the gate back and forth. You didn't have to push and pull the sheep around to put them where you wanted them.

"It was fine," I said, "The way they had it at Mr. Miller's."

"We could have one here."

"You think so?"

"I'm asking you."

Why me, I don't know. With everyone else there. Me, I was just the one who was going to stay around the farm all summer taking care of Jimmy the orphan. But even I knew enough to see how good it was.

"Sure," I said. "Fine."

"Then let's put one up this year," said my father. "Where should we rig it?"

"You asking me?"

He already had turned away. "You figure it out," he said, "while we finish fencing up the pen."

All this, I did not understand. Me? My big brothers and uncles, with the big brains, who could think harder than me, they were the ones going to summer pasture with the flock. Not me. Unless my father was changing his mind. And maybe he was, except that it was too much. Such a thing, that would be a miracle sure. Like the man with the big fish or the one with the bugle. A thing like that was just too much to hope for.

Especially now, when I wanted to take it easy from hoping anymore. To hope so much, it's like carrying what's heavy, like too big a load of wood from the woodpile. And you don't know whether to try and drop some halfway, and you're afraid if you do you'll drop the whole load, and if you don't that you'll drop the whole load anyway before you get to the house. Until your brain gets tired from thinking what to do, and your arms feel like they're ready to fall off. So that the next time you just give up and make two trips instead of one. That's the way I felt about hoping. I didn't want to try anymore.

I just went ahead and looked how to fix this chute and the gate. I took a stick and drew lines on the ground where I thought everything should be. I studied it all over as hard as I could, erasing some of the lines and fixing them better. Then when I had it right I called my father. I pointed out the lines where the fence should be for the chute, and the opening where the sheep should come in and the place for the swinging gate, and all. My father walked up and down, looking close at each line.

"Miguel," he said at last, "that's all right."

"You mean it?"

"Fine."

"I think it will work good," I said.

"With just two or three small changes, it couldn't work better."

He showed me the changes, just little ones. Rubbing out some of the lines in the dirt, he moved the chute over maybe three feet. He made the place where the sheep come in point in a different direction. And he shifted around how the gate was. But otherwise, he left everything just the way I arranged it. And all the time he talked to me as serious as if I were one of the big ones.

That's the second time it happened. And it happened again, too, in the next days, my father asking me what I thought and talking to me like I was one of the others. Then it happened like this, the day the shearers arrived.

We were fixing the floor of the shearing shed, taking out the boards that were broken or had got rotted and putting in new boards to make a nice, clean floor. My father said, "Miguel, hand me one of those planks."

I said, "Which one?"

"As for which one," he looked up from where he was nailing, "I want you to pick out the one that you figure is the best one."

There wasn't much to choose from, just a bunch of boards standing up in the corner. I looked over each board, both sides, and took the one with the least knots, that was the smoothest, so that when it was part of the floor and the men were working on the floor with the wool, the fleeces wouldn't get caught in any splinters. My father looked at the board when I brought it to him and shook his head like something great had happened.

"This is a real fine plank," he said.

"It's pretty good." I didn't see anything so wonderful about it.

"No one could have picked out a better one."

For some days I had been thinking to ask a question. Now I asked it. "Are you making fun out of me?"

"How do I make fun out of you?"

"Well—by talking to me all the time so serious."

My father got a look on his face like he was worried. He put down the board and the hammer, and he lighted a cigarette. "Miguel," he said, "there is this you have to understand. And that is to say only one thing at a time. First you say I make fun out of you. And at the same time you say I speak with you too serious. Such talk mixes me up. You've got to tell me, which is it?"

I tried to figure it out. My father smoked his cigarette and pushed the ashes off the end with his little finger, looking at me. I knew what I meant. But to make fun and be serious all at once, I know it didn't sound right together. Yet if I wasn't ready to go with the others, then why should he talk to me like I *was* one of the others? Unless he was changing his mind. If not he should behave like always, not knowing who brought the plank—whether it was me, Miguel, or somebody else. Except that if he did *that* it would be no good at all. This was better. So why was I making a mixup? Who knows what could be happening?

"I, too," I said. "It mixes me up, too."

"Both of us in the same fix." He blew out a big cloud of smoke, and from his tongue he picked a little piece of tobacco. "What do we do about it?"

"Look, if it's all the same with you, I got to ask a favor."

"Whatever you say."

"Let's forget, I mean—could we forget like I didn't say anything?"

"Whatever you say." My father threw away the cigarette, tossed some nails in his mouth, and went back to hammering. But right then we heard a loud blowing from the horn of an auto, again and again, and we all looked up. It was the Marquez brothers, who every year come to shear our flock. They were turning in from the regular roadway over across the fields, into our own road that leads to the house, two cars, one pulling a trailer.

My father stopped hammering. Everyone stopped what he was doing. Out in the corrals, in the sheds, and in the house. Everyone came out to welcome the Marquez brothers and the others who were their shearing crew.

All of us are glad to see the shearers. One reason is, when they come it is like the time of harvest. Then the wool is clipped and stuffed into long bags, and my father takes these bags on the truck and brings them to Mr. Morrison in Taos. He has a contract which is a promise to bring to Mr. Morrison all the wool when we cut it, and Mr. Morrison has a promise to pay so much money for each pound that my father brings. One year Mr. Morrison promises to pay more for a pound, like one dollar, and one year he promises to pay less, like fifty cents. Why more one year and less the next, I don't know. When I once asked Gabriel, who knows everything pretty good, he said the price of wool is different from time to time, according to how things are. When I asked him what things, he said things in general. So that's the reason, if you ask me why more one year and less the next, I say, "I don't know."

But more or less, whatever, this is the time when if my mother needs a new ironing board, which this year she does, she gets a new ironing board; and Leocadia, for instance, gets a dress, and Pedro, new shoes; and Blasito gets parts for the tractor—all out of the money that comes from Mr. Morrison.

That's one reason why everyone is glad to see the shearers. And the other reason we're glad to see them is that they are always happy.

There are two Marquez brothers. One is Juan, who we call Johnny, and the other is Salvador, who we call Salph. Johnny is round and not so big, and Salph is round and bigger, and with them is always three or four others, this year three. One of the others is always the same, he is Melchior, with a dark face and a little pointy beard. And the rest of the others are always new men, different from year to year, so that my big sisters Tomasita and Leocadia are always interested in seeing what the new ones will look like.

Every year, I have been told, the Marquez brothers and their crew leave their home in Colorado, which is the state north of us, and early in the year around March they go way down to the bottom of Texas, which is the state south of us. Here it is already almost summer, and here they start shearing, first one flock then another, coming north all the time, so that always where they are it is just the same season, almost summer, and there are sheep for them to shear. When they leave us they go north, even above the place where they live in Colorado, until it's no longer almost summer anywhere and there are no more sheep to shear. Then they go home, and in the winter the Marquez brothers run a gas station.

But selling gas, Johnny Marquez once told me, is not so good a life as shearing sheep. Not only is it better to go around the country talking to many different people, he told me, but shearing their sheep seems to make people more satisfied than filling their tank with gas.

Johnny tells me such things because he is my good friend. And this year when he first saw me he treated me fine. He and my father came up the path from the house, each with an arm around the other, talking and laughing. When Johnny saw me, he threw his hands up into the air.

"Miguel, Miguelito!" he yelled. "Look at what's happened. He shoots up like an airplane. In one year, a giant!"

"Hi, Johnny," I laughed because he looked so funny, "How goes?"

"How goes, *hombre*, how goes? Goes one hundred and fifty per cent good with nothing off for cash. But look at him!" he turned to my father. "You got yourself a new hand."

"Ai," said my father. "A good one."

They weren't laughing now, they were talking honest. Johnny winked at me. "What's this bandit of a father paying you in wages? How much?"

"Board and keep," I said.

"That's all?"

"For now," said my father. "We didn't discuss wages when we had our talk. The big thing we decided was that Miguel here should become a regular part of the work this year when school was over."

I was surprised with my father, how good he remembered the way we talked that time at the tractor. What he said was the big thing, that wasn't exactly so. But he did remember.

"Miguel, *hombre*," said Johnny. "Let me tell you about this father of yours. When you talk business with him, don't take chances. Always make sure there's somebody around."

"I did," I said. "There was someone around."

"Indeed there was." My father remembered everything. "Blasito and Padre de Chavez."

"They were on his side." Johnny shook his head like it was no good. "Next time you make a deal, wait till I come around. I'll get you everything you want." And he hit me with his thumb, like we had a secret together.

"Miguel does all right," said my father. "He doesn't need any Juan Marquez to talk for him. He gets what he wants by himself."

"If you don't, Miguel," Johnny hit me again, "you see me. I'll fix it up."

And the two of them went down the path, down to the yard where was the shearing shed. I watched them and I kept on smiling. Because my father remembered the talk at the tractor and how important it was, and you could see that he was thinking about it.

And Johnny, it was good to have him around. The way he called me *hombre* and said how big I was and talked how I was a new hand, which means a regular workman around the place, and my father agreeing with everything he said. And Johnny saying over again how he was going to help me get what I wanted.

It was almost like someone was fixing things up. As if I said my wish to San Ysidro all right, and that he heard me, and was arranging matters in a certain kind of way. Watching Johnny Marquez, it was easy to think of San Ysidro because they look a little alike, round and not so big. And I wondered maybe, if it ever happened San Ysidro would give the job to anybody to work things out here at the Chavez farm, whether he wouldn't pick out a man that

looked like him, the way Johnny Marquez did. I didn't
wonder about this long. I don't know how saints work.
Whether they ever hire anybody to do a job for them, or
what. It might all be foolish what I was wondering, so I
stopped.

But like everybody was happy the shearers had come, I
was especially happy. Except for one thing. Now that they
were here there wasn't much time left. Right after the flock
is sheared, no more than four or five days, then that's the
end. Then the flock leaves for the Sangre de Cristo.

There was only a little time, for me. Maybe not enough
for my father to change his mind.

There was only a little time, for San Ysidro. If he was

really going to do anything. It was no use, I didn't think, to make my wish to him all over again. All I could do was hope that there weren't too many earthquakes and volcanos and floods to keep him busy in other places, so he could put in a little time here at the Chavez place to work things out.

CHAPTER 10

BY THE end of the first day of shearing, there was no question about it. Something *was* happening, and it was something good.

Even at the start, everyone setting up to go to work, you could see how things were going. Like when I got back to the shed. My father was helping Salph Marquez unload shearing tools. He yelled at me without looking around, over his shoulder.

"Miguel! Where've you been? I want you to finish up that last plank."

"I haven't been anywhere," I said.

"Is that any reason you shouldn't nail up the plank?"

"No," I said, because he was right like always. And besides, I was glad to go to work and be busy along with everyone else. I hammered the last plank in the floor good. Except the first three nails I used were the kind that when you don't hit them just right they bend over in the middle.

All around, everyone was in a hurry. Gabriel and Bonifacio filled the big corral with sheep. They yelled and they banged the fences with sticks to hurry the sheep along. Blasito herded a bunch into the yard that was fenced off in front of the shearing shed. It was the first bunch that was going to be sheared. He used the swinging gate I had figured out. It worked good. In back of the shed was Eli, hanging up the first wool bag. This is a very long bag, six feet long, maybe more. It hangs from the top of the wall, the back wall of the shed, where it is tied on to a square frame made of wood that is built on up there, high enough so the bag can hang without touching the ground. Eli was hammering, too. Together, he and I made one big lot of noise.

My grandfather went around to everybody, to tell each one how to do his work. Each one, except the shearers. No one can tell them what to do. They are experts, and they bring with them everything they need. Even their own electricity.

140

That is what is on the trailer they pull, a special gasoline engine to make their own electricity. It is not a large trailer. Not like those you sometimes see that's like a house and people live in it. This is only big enough to hold the gasoline engine with a round shed over it, all painted bright shiny silver and on it the words, SHEARING PLANT.

From the trailer there leads out a thick wire, and Johnny carried the end of it across to the shed. On this end of the wire there is a box with many small holes in it, and into these holes Johnny plugged smaller wires that carry the electricity to the clippers. Hanging from a beam that was part of the roof of the shed, the clippers were at the end of long steel arms with hinges that twist and turn whichever way you want. These clippers were hung up about six feet apart, and there was one for each of the five shearers.

The clippers are exactly the kind that a barber uses, if he is a barber that has clippers which work with electricity. Only these clippers are bigger.

There was a time when everyone clipped by hand, the way my father still does, using scissors with flat blades, to cut away a little bit of wool from a ewe for one reason or another. There are some who still believe to cut by hand is better, Johnny tells me. Especially in the north where it is colder. Up there, some herders think such clippers that work with electricity cut too close, and that not enough wool is left on the sheep to protect the animal against the weather. Maybe they are right, maybe not. There are many things I never thought about. And I guess this is one of them.

But one thing is sure. To cut with clippers that work with electricity is certainly faster. And that's good for the shearers. They get paid for each fleece that they cut, like this year thirty-five cents for each one. So the faster they work, the more money they make. And for a shearer it is important to make all the money he can because every night almost they play cards, and to play so much cards, I hear, you've got to have a lot of money.

Johnny was hanging up the last of the clippers when I finished with the plank.

"Mike," he said, "grab a broom. You better clean this floor pronto, sweep it up. We're almost ready to go."

"I don't know," I looked around for my father, "whether it's me."

"What's you? What's there to know? We can't clip wool on a floor like this. Where's the broom?"

"Maybe he wants someone else should do it."

"Who do you mean he? Your father?" He looked around and yelled. "Hey, Chavez!" My father had gone out to the corral to help herd the first bunch into the pen. He looked around to Johnny.

"How about letting your new hand ride the broom?" yelled Johnny, pointing to me with his head. "Floor's dirty."

My father nodded. "All right with you, Miguel? Can you do it?"

142

"Easy," I said. I reached for the broom close by in the corner.

"Anything at all," Johnny gave me a wink. "Anything you want. Just let me know."

It's a big job. To be the one with the broom. When the fleeces come off the sheep, they lay around the floor before they get tied up. And if they get dirty, with twigs and dirt, Mr. Morrison is disappointed. So to keep the fleeces clean, the way the best quality wool should be, the floor has to be swept all the time in the best and most careful way. Nothing is more important. And yet it was me who was going to do it. For my father to give me a job like this meant that something was happening sure, something good.

I swept as hard as anyone could, sending up clouds of dirt as big as any I ever saw. By then the shearers were doing the last thing before they go to work, and that is to sharpen the blades of the clippers. They sharpen them so fine and thin that even to look at the shiny clippers makes you feel almost your finger is bleeding. The shearers work with little files, smoothing the edge of each separate tooth in their machine. One of them, Melchior, sharpened the blade of his clipper on a small grindstone that turned at the end of an electric motor. Working all together they made a lot of different noises, grinding, scratching, and filing noises.

The sheep just watched. They stood in the pen, chewing their cud, looking at the shearers as if everything going on

143

had nothing to do with them at all. They just watched with lazy eyes while the five shearers filed and scratched away, sharpening their clippers to go to work on them.

It made you want to laugh how proud the sheep looked, proud and not seeing anything, while the shearers were getting ready to give them what for. What I mean, the sheep weren't going to be hurt. No matter how sharp and shiny the clippers. But it looked like something terrible was going to happen. Like sharpening up swords, for a big battle. And the ewes just chewing, too proud to take notice, too proud and lazy to think anything was ever going to happen to them.

It looked funny. The ewes didn't believe it could ever be different from the way it had been. When everything that was done was for their good. The way we fed them. And kept them warm. And brought them to water. And kept the coyotes away. But never once did they ever look thankful. Instead, they did everything to cross you up. They ran away. And said no to their own children. And wouldn't feed the lambs. And always they went in the wrong direction from where you wanted to drive them.

Now, what was being done was for the good of somebody else—our family and the shearers. And they didn't believe it. Each one of them stood looking like one of those high society ladies you see in my mother's books, all dressed up and smiling at the top of the page as if the whole rest of the world was off somewhere making a fancy sandwich to

144

bring to them on a tray. They didn't know it, but they were in for one big time with the clippers getting sharper and sharper. They stood there, those ewes, just chewing away.

I had to laugh and I did. It was like getting paid back for all the troubles I had. With the sheep. With everything. Trying to get up to the mountains and all. It was only the big ones who got sheared. The lambs, they were put outside the pen. Only the big ones, who gave so much trouble to the young ones, only they were in for it. No matter how much they chewed, no matter how proud and lazy they looked, they were in for it.

My father pushed the last sheep in the pen and closed the swinging gate.

"Full up," he yelled to Johnny.

"Let's go. *Vamonos!*" Johnny turned to Salph who was standing by the engine. "Let her ride!"

Salph cranked the engine once. It sputtered, then it roared. All the clipping machines started to clatter, to hum, and to whine. The five shearers like an army advanced on the sheep. And the ewes still stood and chewed and looked proud.

Five stopped chewing. Five were caught by their hind legs. Five ewes were being pulled. The shearers flipped them over on their backs. Like sacks, the shearers dragged the ewes under the shed. They lifted the ewes and tossed them around. They bounced them on the floor and sat the ewes up. The shearers slipped the heads of the ewes between their knees and held them tight. The shearing was started.

It was better than the dancing on San Ysidro Day to watch the shearers work. For a little while the five of them all kept in time with each other—the clippers, the arms and the heads of the shearers all doing the same thing at once. First, with the ewes sitting up, the heads held by the shearer's knees, Johnny and Salph, Melchior and all started to clip down the belly of the sheep. Then all of them let go of the heads of the ewes, and turned the animal over on its side. Holding the ewe's head down with one knee, they started the long cut, the clippers starting at the tail of the sheep, whining in a long curve right up the backs of each ewe up to behind their ears.

The fleece came off in strips now, the way you husk an ear of corn, showing the white wool underneath but all in one piece. That's part of being an expert, to get the fleece off in one whole piece, rolling it off their back as if it were a rug. When they finish with the back, the shearers work on the head, between the ears and around the eyes and the nose. It is very difficult to keep the wool from here to remain a part of the whole piece. It comes off in little bits, and these little bits are called tag wool and such wool is gathered up separately. By the time they finished with the first ewe, the shearers got out of time with each other because some were faster than the others, like Johnny and Melchior who worked the fastest. From then on it wasn't

146

like a dance any more. Just hard work, everyone going as fast as they could.

The shearers must work in a hurry, in order to make all that money. And to do all the jobs besides the cutting that has to be done, we work in a hurry to keep up with the shearers.

My father and grandfather tied the fleeces. This is a special job for which you have to be an expert almost as much as the clipping itself. First the fleece is spread out on the floor, with the dirty part, which was the outside wool of the sheep, underneath on the floor. Then you shake the fleece a little, to get rid of whatever dirt is hanging on and to ruffle up the nice white part that is on top. After that you bunch it around and wrap it so that only the white part shows; and when you get a nice tight bundle, you tie it up with string that hangs in bunches from the roof.

If you do the job properly then each bundle of wool looks good, and Mr. Morrison is very satisfied, and next year you get a better price for each pound because the wool looked like it was such good quality. My father and grandfather are experts at tying the wool up like this.

The string they use is special, too. It looks like just ordinary string, like cord, only it's not. It's made out of paper wound tight together to look like cord. And it's better because regular ordinary string can shed the hard hairs it's made of, and if the hairs get into the wool, and the wool gets made into a stocking, and then you feel an itch on your ankle, that's what it could be.

Another thing about the string is that it's used to keep score for the shearers, to keep count how many sheep they clip. At the start Johnny and Salph, Melchior and the others, each one takes a hundred strings and hangs them up in a bunch near where he works. If my father ties up a fleece of Johnny's he takes a string from Johnny's bunch, and if it's Melchior's fleece he takes a string from the bunch hanging near Melchior. This way, by counting the strings, one knows how many sheep each man has clipped. All you do is subtract the number of strings from one hundred, which is easy enough simple arithmetic, and then you know. And when the whole bunch of strings is gone that's even simpler, it means the shearer has finished one hundred ewes exactly. Most of them can finish one bunch of strings in a day, some even more. It takes them only four, five or six minutes to clip a sheep.

With five new fleeces to tie and five new sheep to be dragged to the clippers every few minutes, you can see that no one had a chance to stand around. Every little while you'd hear one of the shearers yelling, "Sheep up! Sheep up!" meaning that new ones had to be herded into the pen. Gabriel and Bonifacio were working as wranglers, keeping the pen full of sheep to be sheared and getting the clipped ewes out of the pen to the lambs that were waiting outside.

This part is very important too, and a little funny besides. Because no lambs are brought into the pen. They are separated from their mothers, and they crowd around in a gang watching what's happening through the fences.

What's happening must look, to a lamb, like something terrible is going on, the way the ewes are grabbed and yanked and twisted up in the air and bounced down in a sitting position. All crumpled up this way, the ewe with her wool on looks fat and comfortable, like the big over-stuffed chair we have in our sitting room.

But soon, once the shearers get started, it gets to look like the overstuffed chair was having its stuffings pulled out, the way the white wool starts to come off in bunches and rolls until you can't see anything but just stuffing laying around the floor covering up the sheep's head and feet and all. That must look strange enough to the lamb.

But when the clippers stop whining, and the fleece is off and the shearer kicks the ewe back onto its feet, that must look strangest of all. Instead of a big, comfortable, wooly-looking mother, a new kind of naked, bony-looking animal, all corners and bumps, stands there instead. The ewe doesn't mind. It makes her feel happy. With the summer coming and the weather already hot, she likes to get rid of her coat. It makes her frisky and glad.

But to the lambs looking through the fence it must look like their mother disappeared someplace. Even when the ewes are put outside again, and the lambs can take a close look, sometimes even then a lamb won't know its mother. It will just stand there, looking at this new kind of skinny-looking animal and bawl its lungs out like in two minutes the whole world was going to explode.

It's important that you get them together quick. If a ewe

149

and her lamb are separated too long the lamb gets too hungry. And it might lead to where they don't recognize each other at all anymore, even by the smell. And if that happens then the job is really hard because now there are no numbers to help. The numbers get sheared off the ewe along with the wool. So Gabriel and Bonifacio have to watch close to see that each lamb gets to its mother right away. This is their job, too, as well as keeping the pen filled when the shearers yell, "Sheep up! Sheep up!"

I kept up with all the rest, so busy with my broom that Johnny started to call me "Twister!"

What he meant was that wherever I went, there was always a cloud of dust moving around on account of how hard I swept, such a cloud that it looked like a sandstorm. And when there is a sandstorm they call it a twister. That's why when Johnny called me, he'd yell, "Hey, Twister, over here. Sweep me out of here. Clean it up!"

And once when I went over to clean up where he was working he called over to my father. "This new hand of yours, Twister, he's worth two men. You're lucky, Chavez, to get him. A man like that."

"Lucky?" My father shook his head. "When we need a good man, we don't depend on luck. We raise them." That's what he said, my father, without a smile, serious.

It made me work twice as hard. In addition to sweeping I picked up the tag wool, all the little bits that were laying around. These I put into a separate bag that lay in the corner. Because it was dirty and in little pieces, the tag wool

150

has to be delivered in a special bag so it will not be mistaken for the good wool. This, too, was part of my job, gathering all the tag wool in the right bag. And everyone left it for me to do, handing me bits or kicking hunks of wool over for me to pick up. In the same way they left it to the shearers to work the clippers. Something was happening and I was getting to be like everyone else.

Even Pedro saw how it was going. He was taking the dope can around where it was needed, which is a can full of some kind of linament you put on the sheep when the shearers clip a little too close, sometimes, and maybe make a scratch or a little cut. It's not hard to do, just to hold the dope can, and most of the time Pedro could take it easy, sitting on the fence watching, which is what he likes to do best.

But this time, he came over and said, "Hello, Twister," in a voice like Johnny Marquez.

I spoke like Johnny, too. "Hi, Pete. How are things doing and what's news?"

For the last couple of weeks, we hadn't been together, Pedro and me, like we used to. I didn't tell him about what happened at the tractor, or about the wish I made to San Ysidro, or anything. And Pedro, too, he didn't talk about the plan either. Maybe he forgot by now, but I think he figured it all worked out so good that I was going for sure, along with the others, this summer. Now he didn't make fun anymore, talking like Johnny Marquez, but in his own voice.

"Is it hard?" he asked me.

"What?"

"Being big like the rest and so busy?"

"No," I said. "It's not so hard."

"You want me to help?"

"If you like."

"It's not what I like. It's only if you want. What I like is doing nothing and looking."

"Then why not?" I said. "I can work by myself."

"It sure is a good name, what they call you now." Pedro shook his head. "Twister." Then he went away and climbed back on the fence.

By the end of the day, when the sun was going down, half the flock was all finished being sheared.

"Better than a year ago." My father was tying up the last fleece. "Isn't that so, Johnny? We didn't get anywhere near this much done the first day last year."

"Only one reason for that." Johnny hit me with his thumb again. "Got some new men around here who know how to work."

They both laughed, and I laughed too. I walked with them and the others back to the house, everyone making jokes. I wished I could remember some jokes to tell but I never can. So I just laughed with the others. On the veranda my mother laid out basins and pails of water so we could all get cleaned up for supper. I got washed up with the rest. But I couldn't comb my hair like they did because my hair is short, just stubby, like a field that's been grazed over.

It wasn't only in the shearing sheds that it was busy all day. In the house, too, they worked hard, my mother and Tomasita and Leocadia. It had to be the best supper. Because the shearers ate at many farms. And at each farm they are supposed to say, "Mama mia, this is the best, the absolute best yet!" So if you don't give them a chance to say this by serving the best supper, that's a disgrace. That's why she and my sisters, they prepare as if everyone's birthday had come together on the same day.

When we got into the kitchen, the table was laid out with only our best plates, and the knives and forks we only get to see on Christmas or Easter. It looked fine. And on the stove there wasn't even one small part that wasn't covered by some kind of food cooking, a crowd of pots and pans smelling the place up good.

The big table in our kitchen is not so big for as many people as this. My mother and sisters they wait to eat until after the men finish, and so do the children, Faustina and Pedro. I waited, too. But I didn't go away. It's good to stand around and hear what the shearers have to tell, because that way you get to hear things you can't find out about any other way. I stood at the door along with Faustina and Pedro, while the men sat down and rubbed their hands together the way they always do when they're going to eat, and Tomasita and Leocadia started to bring the food from the stove where my mother was piling it on dishes.

Then what happened, if it wasn't a miracle, was something just as good.

153

Mr. Juan Marquez stopped from reaching across the table for a biscuit, and he turned to where I was standing.

"Ai Miguel, what're you doing there?"

"Me? Just standing. Waiting."

"Aren't you hungry?"

"It's not a question of being hungry. It's a question of everybody getting squeezed."

"Who's squeezed? What's squeezed?" He moved over his chair until there was a space of three, four inches. "Look, plenty of room. C'mon."

"It's not only squeezed. There's also the question of my father."

"What? Your father?" At that moment, my father, who sat next to Johnny, was talking to Melchior across the table. Johnny punched him in the shoulder. "Chavez, what is this? Your new hand, ain't he going to eat with the rest of the men?"

"Who, Miguel?" My father turned. "Why not? Of course. Get a stool, Mickey. Get in here."

So my father shifted over his chair, too. And I got a stool. There was just enough room at the table. I put down the stool and sat down on it right at the table. Leocadia reached across with a plate and a knife and fork of my own. I didn't believe what was going on.

Because this was the first time. It had never happened before at any other shearing. No, never before at any time when there were a lot of men who had to eat first did I ever get to sit down along with them to eat first, too. This

154

was as good, any day, as bringing a man out of a whale. You could see now why Saint Ysidro was such an expert. He couldn't have told my father what to do, or grandfather, because they had already said no. He couldn't tell any one of the family, because what my father or grandfather says, goes. It had to be somebody from outside, and who was better than Johnny who was our old friend that everybody liked? And the way Johnny fixed everything, San Ysidro could not have found anyone better.

What it all meant was this. I said it all right to San Ysidro. He heard my wish, and it was all turning out all right.

"Wake up!" The way Johnny pushed me I almost fell off the stool. "With these wolves, you better get something quick or you'll starve sure."

"There's enough." My mother laughed. "Enough for a dozen Miguels."

She was right. In the middle of the table there was a big plate with *gallina rellena*, turkey stuffed with meat and *piñon* nuts and a little taste of cinnamon, then there was this big bowl of *chili colorado con carne*, a stew that was made to taste good with red chili. Then, on one side of this, was a pot of *frijoles machacados*, mashed up *bolita* beans, and on the other side a potato loaf made with eggs and garlic and bacon. Then there were a lot of little dishes, one with sweet chili sauce, and another with *guacamole* salad which is made out of avocadoes and tomatoes and things, and another with peach preserves and then a bowl with

cole slaw. There were two kinds of bread, the *bollitos* my
mother bakes which is a roll that is fat and round and
tortillas which is flat but also round. There were two kinds
of angel food cake, one chocolate and the other vanilla but
only one kind of pie, just apple.

I had a good time. I was hungry, and there were so many
good things to eat I hardly had time to listen. But there
was so many good stories to hear, about all the sheepherders
up and down the Rio Grande Valley, I didn't hardly want
to waste time eating. I got along as best I could doing
both, eating and listening, and feeling good.

Each one tried to tell a better story than the other. My
father told about one time in Penāsco and when everyone

stopped laughing, Johnny said "That reminds me of one time in Bernalillo." And when he told what happened and everyone stopped laughing at that, Salvador said, "That reminds me of one time in Silver City." And after they finished laughing at his story, Melchior said, "That reminds me of one time in Questa," and this was some kind of story about a garter that was purple and pink which made my sister Leocadia laugh so hard she had to leave the kitchen.

Then I remembered a joke that Juby told me, and before I knew it, I said, "That reminds me of one time in the school at Los Cordovas." And everyone stopped quiet and looked at me. I was surprised how quiet. I didn't feel very much like going on. But, what else could I do?

I swallowed what was in my mouth, and I said it as fast as I could. "There was this fellow in Los Cordovas who told this other fellow on the way to the school, 'Last night in the middle of the night it rained cats and dogs,' and this other fellow said, 'How do you know it rained cats and dogs?' and this first fellow said, 'This morning when I came out of my house, in front of the house I found a poodle.' That's all."

Well, you never heard anything like it. How they laughed! They all understood the way I said it, and it turned out to be the best story of all. My brother Blasito across the way, he laughed so much he fell off his chair, and that made everybody laugh even more. When Gabriel

157

helped him back into his seat Blasito was still laughing, and what's more, hiccuping. So everybody just kept on laughing. I never felt so good.

I guess it was the best supper I ever had.

CHAPTER 11

AND now what there is to explain is how the worst thing happened, and then how the best thing happened, and then how everything got mixed up, what was good and what was bad.

The worst thing happened the next morning.

Just to look at, the morning was all right. Or even, to tell the truth, it was a nice morning. The sun was shining and the shadows were long and heavy when we came out of the house. The sky was blue and big like there was more of it around than usual, more clear sky thin as deep water all around. Over the mountains there was clouds looking like a flock of clouds grazing around up there, big and little ones. And over the house, there was a couple of little ones, tramp clouds, like orphans. The Sangre de Cristo, they looked closer than I ever saw them before. Or maybe that was just because of the way I felt.

I felt good that morning when we all went out to finish the shearing. I could still almost taste last night's supper in my mouth, the food and the jokes and everything. When we all walked out together, the others finishing their cigarettes after breakfast, my grandfather told me to hang up the bag for the wool. The rest of the unshorn sheep had to be herded from the fields, where they had grazed all night, into the corral. All the other hands had to go out to round them up and bring them in. So it was up to me, my grandfather said, to hang up the big sack. Me, that is, and Uncle Eli.

I was glad to do this because hanging the sack, after all, is an important job which you don't ask anyone at all to do and which I had never been asked to do before. I knew how it worked, though, from watching.

First, Uncle Eli and I, we got this iron hoop, like a hoop off a barrel only thick and solid, and this hoop we put around the top outside the opening of the sack. Then we turned over the cloth of the sack, which is burlap, we turned it over the hoop all the way around. All that's left is to take some nails, which you use like they were pins, to fasten the turned-over burlap to the rest of the sack so that the hoop is all covered over and it can't fall off.

Once you do this, it's very easy to hang the sack. All you do then is to go up on the wall of the shed where is nailed this square wooden frame and drop the bottom of the empty sack through the frame. But the opening of the sack can't go through because the hoop is bigger than the wooden square and it rests on the square letting the sack hang down at its full length, six or seven feet. That's all there is to it.

But once we got the sack hung up, Uncle Eli said, "Stay up there, Miguelito. We'll get started and sack up these fleeces from yesterday."

Down below there was a bin into which the fleeces are put by the men who tie them up, my father and grandfather. A dozen or so were left over from the afternoon before, covered by a tarpaulin to keep them from the wet and the dew during the night. Eli took off the tarp and started to hand up the fleeces to me standing high up where I was, on the wooden frame on top of the sack. I dropped the fleeces into the sack, one after another, as Eli handed them to me.

By this time the first bunch had been herded into the yard in front of the shearing shed, the clippers were working, the shearing was started. And through the window that is in the back of the shed more fleeces were already starting to come into the bin where Eli was. He kept handing them up to me. I kept dropping them into the sack.

I saw that my brother Blasito was sweeping with the broom, which was the job I did the day before. So I just stayed up on top there, sacking the wool. If anything, this is even a more important kind of work than sweeping, to stand way up on top there to take the fleeces the shearers had cut and my father had tied, and sack them up so we could take them to Mr. Morrison. I never thought I'd be doing this for years yet. But no one said I shouldn't, so there I was up on top, sacking the wool. And by this time the fleeces were coming through the window pretty fast, and no one took any notice who was doing the work as long as it was getting done. Eli didn't have any more time to hand me the fleeces. He started throwing them up to me.

It was easy to catch them. And it was nothing at all to drop them in the sack. But this is not the important part of sacking the wool.

The important part is that the wool has to be packed tight. It must be stamped down so hard and solid that the sack gets to look like one big round sausage. It is not difficult to do. You wait until the fleeces pile up and then you step in the middle of the bag and stamp up and down and jump with all your might until the wool is hard beneath your feet. You don't have to be afraid the bag will tear; it's made out of the best burlap, the strongest kind, and can hold even the biggest men, who are usually the ones that do the sacking.

So there I was up on top. Fleeces flying up from Uncle Eli. Everybody as busy and working as fast as they could,

162

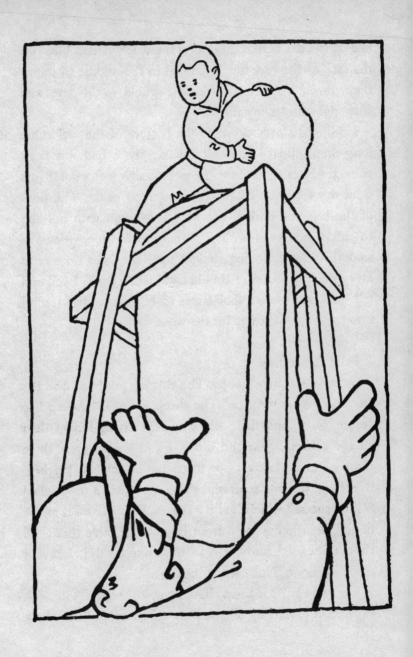

like on the day before. And soon the wooly fleeces filled up the sack to the very top. I stepped in the middle to stamp them down. And it was like the whole world gave way from right under my feet.

I dropped slowly down to the bottom of the sack. One long drop, and then a soft bump. There had not been enough fleeces to hold me up, not enough soft wool. I just went down, slow, and there was nothing to do. The sides of the bag, the burlap, was hard and rough with nothing to catch, not even with fingernails. Like going down a smooth tunnel standing straight up. There was no way to save myself. And yell, I couldn't yell. How could I yell and tell everyone what a fool I was to be falling that second into the bag which was for the wool?

I didn't yell.

I didn't breathe.

Outside nothing stopped. The clippers went on. And the gasoline engine went on. The sheep went on bawling like before. One lamb there was who kept crying louder than all the others, again and again. From the shearers there came a shout, "Sheep up, sheep up!" Someone laughed. And there was one somewhere singing. It was a song called "Chiapenecas" which is also a dance. They played it at the fiesta. The singing came from far away, outside there. All these noises, I heard them in the same second. I myself made no noise. Not even to breathe.

I looked up. As if I was climbing up the rough cloth with my eyes, I looked up all the little crisscrosses of the cloth, and at the end I reached the top. Way up, high above me, I saw the sky, still blue like this morning but no longer big and wide. An eye, a round eye it was, way up at the end of the tunnel, still blue and with one tramp cloud, an orphan cloud.

I breathed. And then, *Madre Dios*, a shadow went past the eye. It was a fleece. And right away another. Eli, without looking, he was still throwing fleeces up to me and I wasn't there. The fleeces were going right over the top of the bag. Another came and another. And no one to catch them. I stretched my hands, high, high, knowing I couldn't stretch high enough but stretching up anyway if only to beg they should stop. But over it came, another shadow. I grabbed at the bag around me, wishing I was a cat with claws. But there was nothing, the cloth was too tight and hard to grab. And still it came, another fleece sailing over the opening of the bag way up above.

There was a shout. "Miguel!"

Someone yelled. "What are you doing with the fleeces, Eli? Throwing them away?"

"Eli!"

"What?" That was Eli. "What's wrong? Well, what do you know! Miguel! Where is he? Miguel!"

The fleeces stopped. And everywhere, shouts. For me, Miguel.

"Ai, Miguel!"

"Miguel, where are you?"

"Where'd he go, Miguel?"

"Miguel!"

"Did you see Miguel?"

"Hey Miguel, Miguel! Speak up! Miguel!"

I didn't say anything. I wished only that my name was something different from Miguel. Alexander, Joe, Babaloo —anyone, except me.

"Miguel!"

It was my big brother Blasito who thought of it first. "Maybe he fell into the bag?"

Said one of the shearers, "Yeah, you better look in the bag."

Eli yelled, "Miguel, are you in there? Answer me, Miguel!"

"He's in there all right." It was Salph. "How do you like that? The boy fell in the bag."

"What do you think?" Everyone started to laugh, they roared. "Miguel's in the bag!"

Then I heard Johnny Marquez. My friend, Mr. Marquez. The one who looked like San Ysidro. Mr. Marquez, who I thought had come to the Chavez farm on account San Ysidro asked him to fix things up for me. Johnny was laughing harder than all the rest.

"Did you ever see anything like that Twister, Miguel?" He hit somebody on the back. I could hear it. "He gets tired of being a big man up there. So he jumps back into the sack and goes to sleep."

They screamed and yelled and laughed at how funny this was. There were also other jokes. When I looked up

again it was just in time to see the face of my father come into the round blue hole way up there, above my head.

"He's here all right!" yelled my father. He looked down at me again. "What in Heaven's name, Miguel, do you think you're doing down there?"

I was breathing. That's all. But there was no need to tell him this.

"Is this any time to start playing games, hide and seek, like you were a little boy?"

When he said this I stopped breathing again.

He put down his hand. It hung there, big fingers and a big thumb, right in front of my nose.

"Come on, Miguel, let me get you out of this!" The thumb and one of the other fingers, they snapped. They made a loud noise, one, two, three times. "Miguel! Give me your hand. Up!"

I went back to breathing. But I didn't take the hand. Even when the fingers snapped again, loud and angry. I didn't want to go up. I wanted to stay down here, where there was a shadow and it was dark.

Out there it was bright and blue and the sky was big, and if I went up everyone could see from all around that it was me, Miguel. I could only stay down here, at the bottom of this tunnel. The fingers snapped again, and still I didn't move. The only miracle I wanted now was that when I got pulled out I should be somebody different from who I was—Alexander, or Joe, or Babaloo. Not me, Miguel.

My father was angry. "Give me your hand, Miguel, or I'll pull you out by the scruff of your neck. Now come on! Up!"

The big finger, upside down, shook at me. I put up my hands and took the hand hanging there in front of my nose. As soon as I did, my father grabbed me by the wrist.

"Games," he said. "At a time like this."

He lifted me up into the bright day. He dropped me over the side. I fell into the dirt at the bottom of the sack. Up above my father yelled, "Gabriel, get over here! And get those fleeces out of the rubbish. Come on, hombres, we got a day's shearing yet to do."

I didn't look around to see who watched me. They were

168

stopping to laugh and the clipping machines started up again, loud. I sat there in the dirt without moving because there was nowhere I could think of to go. When I fell I picked up a handful of dirt and now I let the dirt go out of my hand, a little bit at a time. After a while I looked up, and there was Gabriel high up in the sky, sticking out of the sack. He was stamping down the wool with all his might, and at the same time he caught the fleeces that Eli was throwing up to him. He turned round and round up there, pushing down the wool solid and tight the way it should be, Gabriel with all the blue and the clouds behind him.

I heard Johnny Marquez. "Sheep up!" That was him, his voice. For a second I thought to get mad at Johnny Marquez. But in the next second I thought not. Because there was no reason to be mad at Mr. Marquez. He had not given to me any promise. It was not him who said that he was arranging anything for San Ysidro. It was me, Miguel, who figured that out. My idea. All of it, everything was just something I decided in my own mind. About the miracle. And there wasn't any miracle. About San Ysidro hearing my wish. And San Ysidro he didn't hear anything, he didn't know I was alive, San Ysidro. About me becoming part of the whole crew. And all it was, I swept with the broom. About me being a new hand, with a new name, Twister. And all it was, a joke. About sitting down first with the men who ate first. A joke, too, that's all it was.

Ai! It was only me, Miguel, running here and there with

169

my eyes closed, like a lizard, poking into where I shouldn't go, pushing where I couldn't get. Me, Miguel, with my numbers, and my big plan and my lost sheep, all it got me was to the bottom of a deep hole and my father up above talking to me like I was a little boy playing hide-and-go-seek. Me, Miguel, the one who wanted to go to the Sangre de Cristo Mountains, if I could have stayed at the bottom of the hole that would have been good enough for me.

Whatever dirt there was left in my hand, I threw it away.

I made myself small and I got up. I walked away from the shearing shed across the yard, without looking back. No one called me to look back, and there was no one I wanted to see. And in this way I was able to reach the gate which led to the path that went to the house.

And then there was Jimmy, who came running up behind me. I was glad to see him. We went together behind the house and sat down in the shade. Jimmy nibbled at my ear with his soft tight lips, and I rubbed his coat hard the way he likes it. It was good to be with him, that lamb Jimmy, who didn't know anything and who didn't care. The sooner the men left with the flock and left us alone for the summer, the better I'd like it.

After a while, Pedro came and sat down with us.

"Hello, Twister," he said.

"My name ain't Twister."

"Miguel, then."

"My name's Babaloo."

"Why you mad at me?"

170

"Who's mad?"

"I was just looking to tell you, I heard."

"On top of old smoky," I sang the song, just the first line. Pedro waited till I sang it over three times.

"Was bad what happened, hey?" he asked.

"Bad? What's bad about it? Nothing's so bad?"

"I'm glad to hear," he said. "That's what I hoped. You're smart enough, you'd know how to fix it."

"I'm smart enough," I said. "Smart enough to be the smartest man in the whole Rio Grande Valley and in Colorado."

"You know what I mean," Pedro shook his head, "that plan you fixed up. You know, the one that works so good?"

"There isn't any plan."

"The one, you know, about going up in the mountains this summer?"

"Who? Me? Who's going up into the mountains? They can stay right over there, for all I want out of them. They can look as big as they want, and I'll go ahead doing what I feel like, too. And if you think I'm worrying about San Ysidro, either, then all I can tell you is, you're crazy."

"Who?" asked Pedro.

"San Ysidro, that's who. And the mountains! And you! If you ever thought I did have a plan, then all I got to say is you're crazy."

"Me, Miguel?" Pedro looked at me in big surprise.

"Who's Miguel? I'm not me, Miguel. Or me, Pedro. Or me, Faustina. Or me, anybody. And as for you, why

171

don't you get out of here and go someplace and take a walk?"

For a while we just sat there and we didn't say anything. At last Pedro said, "You mean it?"

"I mean it," I said.

So Pedro got up from where we were sitting and went away. And after a while Jimmy and I went down to the river, and we followed it for a long way until we were far from the house. Then I sat around watching Jimmy eat grass, which he was learning to do pretty good.

That's the way it was on the second day of the shearing. That's the way the worst thing happened and it was shown to me that I was not going to go to the Sangre de Cristo Mountains.

And the best thing that could happen, that didn't happen until a week later.

I wasn't around the place much that week. But I heard how things went. The shearing was good and everybody was satisfied how it came out. The average clip was better than ten pounds of wool for each ewe. That's all right. And when Johnny Marquez left, he told my mother to say goodbye to me for him. "Tell Twister," he said, "if everything doesn't work out okay with Chavez, he can always come be a hand with me. I'll teach him how to shear." It was one of his jokes, I guess, and he didn't mean anything by it one way or the other.

There was a lot to do that week, from what I heard. They had to truck all the bags of wool to Mr. Morrison. And a lot of the days there wasn't anyone around the house, because my mother and sisters, they were in town buying things at the store, things that were needed. And with the flock there was hard work, getting them ready for what was to come soon, to leave for the summer. They were sprayed with some kind of cleaning dope, this was to take care of the ticks and bugs and things that were left on them after their wool was sheared off. Then they had to be branded by using an iron with paint on it to make the brand we use, which is B and C, for Blas Chavez, only the B is backwards so that it looks like ꓭC . And then the lambs had to have their tails docked, which means shortened, and this is done by one sharp cut that doesn't hurt at all. And at the same time the lambs that were growing up to be rams had to be cut so they wouldn't grow up to be rams anymore. All this happened that week.

As for me, I went fishing. From the first thing in the morning until it got good and dark, which was pretty late along about then, the middle of the month of June. I went fishing because there were a lot of fish in the river and there was no use wasting them. They were easy to catch, by hand in some places or by line; and so I went out every day because what good are a lot of trout unless they are caught, and besides I like to fish. And whichever way you look at it, to tell the truth, what was the use of hanging around anyway?

Then, one afternoon, happened the best thing that could. I was fishing in a pool that's down near the wooden bridge that's on the road from Ranchitos. I was a little tired of fishing by then, if you want to know, day after day, all the time. And all the fish I'd caught that day was three. I had them on the hook of a branch I picked up. I didn't care they were only three. Because most of the time I just sat there on a rock in the sun, thinking. Not about anything in particular—just thinking about things, how they were. About how there were things you could do something about. And others, other things that you couldn't do anything about at all. Like the way lambs get born, and the way people get to go places they have to go, mountains and different places like that. That's the way I was thinking.

Then, I heard screaming. Loud screaming in a high screechy voice. Where we live most of the faraway sounds you hear is sheep baaing, or cattle bawling, or a truck motor or a gunshot, and not so often screaming. So I was interested. And far away on top of a hill, on the way to our house, I saw this jumping up and down that turned out to be a little girl jumping up and down, that turned out to be Faustina jumping up and down. So I picked up my fish and went to have a closer look, Faustina screaming and jumping all the time till I got close enough to hear what she was saying.

Well, when you get close enough to Faustina to hear what she is saying, most of the time it don't help very much because she's not saying anything except a word, her own private kind of word. And that's the way it was now.

174

The word she was screaming was a new word she had for the last couple of days, GalgoGalgalena.

I crossed the river on stones and waited until she got over her fit, jumping and screaming, and then I yelled up to her. "What's the matter?"

"GalgoGalgalena," she yelled and gave a couple of more jumps.

"What else?"

"In two days you got to go with the rest of them when all the others leave to take the sheep up into the mountains, because that's what father said you got to do."

"Don't go way," I yelled back to her. "Stay right where you are. I can't hear good."

You never know with Faustina what she's talking about, and for all you know, sometimes what she says makes sense. I got about half way up the hill before I stopped.

"What're you trying to say?" I yelled up to her. "Speak slow."

"You gotta go with the others."

"What others?"

"The men and the sheep."

"When do you mean I gotta go?" Sometimes Faustina talks about things that got to happen hundreds of years from now.

"Tomorrow and then the next day, day after tomorrow. That's when."

"Go where? Faustina, go where?"

175

"To the mountains. To the Sangre de Cristo Mountains."

"Sangre de Cristo." I said it pulling in a big long breath all at the same time. "Sangre de Cristo!" I said it, leaving the breath out in one big shout. I dropped the fishing pole and swung away my fish and started up that hill after Faustina.

After a dozen steps I stopped. You can't be too careful with Faustina, never too sure. I stopped and asked her, "Who said so?"

"Father just said so. Back at the house. Everybody's back at the house talking. And father said this year it's time for Miguel to go. Miguel got to go this year."

I didn't shout or anything. I ran up to the top of the hill where Faustina stood, running very carefully. I wanted to get close to her. And hold her. To get her to say everything over again, to make sure. But when I got close to her, she started to walk away backwards. She wouldn't let me grab her. We walked toward the house this way, her going backwards and me following.

"You're making fun, Faustina," I said.

"No I ain't," she said. "GalgoGalgalena."

"But you remember, father said no, I couldn't go. How does it happen that now he say I got to go?"

"It happens, that's all. A letter came, and everybody stood around talking about the letter, and when I got there father was saying well it looks like Miguel gets what he wants. He's got to be the one who goes with the flock this year and that's what father said, I tell you, that's what he said."

We kept walking along, Faustina backwards, me following.

"What kind of letter?"

"The best kind. Paper all white and folded over, the kind that crinkles."

If this could happen, anything could happen. So I asked. "Did it say anything in the letter about San Ysidro?"

All of a sudden, she started to yell. "San Ysidro, Galgoleno. GalgoGalgoleno."

"Faustina, it's all a joke, isn't it? A joke?"

"Who says it's a joke. It ain't no joke." She screamed. "It's a GalgoGasolino." And she turned and started running for the house. I chased right after her. And when we came around the edge of the sheds, I could see them, the whole family going into the house from where they were standing in front of the porch.

My father was the last, and when I came through the gate onto the path, I yelled and he turned around and waited for me while Faustina ran into the house after the others.

My father waited without speaking until I caught my breath and was able to speak myself. He looked down at me and he looked serious.

"Faustina," I spoke when I had enough breath, "she told me just now about something you said. About me and what you wanted me to do with the flock. Yes?"

"Like what?" asked my father.

"Like when the flock goes up to pasture, and the others go along, and the sheep have to go to the mountains for the summer, and there are those who go and those who stay, that I got to be one of those who go. Am I? Must I go?"

My father said something very simple. I never thought it could be that simple. He said, "Yes."

"I mean to the Sangre de Cristo. I'm going up into the Sangre de Cristo Mountains for the whole summer with the sheep? Me?"

It was no mistake. It was the same as before, simple. My father said, "Yes."

"Well," I spoke quiet because my father looked so serious. "I'm glad."

"I, too, am glad, Miguel, since this is what you wish. I am glad that you are coming with us."

And that's the way the best thing that could happen, did happen. It happened, the best thing, on this one afternoon just a week after I fell into the sack.

And then, right away, the next minute, it happened that everything got mixed up, what was good and what was bad.

I wanted to know how anything like this best thing could ever get to be, so I asked my father, "Faustina, she said there was a letter."

My father nodded his head the way you say, yes. Then he bent down and picked up a stone. He kept throwing the stone up and down in his hand as he talked to me.

"Yes," he said. "There was a letter. The letter came today."

"That's what Faustina said." My father kept throwing the stone and catching it. "There wasn't anything in the letter about San Ysidro, or anything like that?"

"San Ysidro?" My father looked at me surprised. "No. Why should there be anything in it about San Ysidro, in this kind of a letter?"

"I don't know. I just thought. What I mean is, how does a thing like this happen, that I should go this year?"

"Gabriel can't go, that's why."

"Faustina didn't tell me. Something's wrong with Gabriel?"

"He has to go away."

"Not for all summer? Gabriel?"

My father nodded again, yes, and kept tossing the stone. "Gabriel has to go away for a long time. For years, Miguel. Two years, at least."

"What's happened? What's he done, Gabriel?"

"Done? He hasn't done anything. Except to grow to be nineteen years old and to graduate high school, that's all. So now he has to go into the army to train to be a soldier."

"That's what was in the letter?"

"Yes." Up and down went the stone. "We didn't expect such a letter until after the summer. It came like a surprise, this morning."

"What?" I said.

"What do you mean, what? Why—what?"

"It's just to hear everything over again. That's why I said, what."

"You don't understand? What's there to say over again? Didn't you hear?" It wasn't that my father was angry. He was just in a hurry to go away.

So I said, "Yes, I heard. A letter came which means Gabriel has to go be a soldier, and that's why I can go to the mountains. I understand."

My father threw the stone up for me to catch. And still looking at him, not the stone, I caught it.

"That's all," he said as I caught the stone, and he left me to go into the house.

"There's only one thing," I said, and my father turned at the door to hear what it was. "I'm sorry that I was glad."

"Always two things, eh, Miguel?" My father smiled. "Sorry and glad. Always trying to say two things at once." And he banged the screen door behind him.

I looked at the stone that he left me. I tossed it the way he did. To throw it up and catch it was easy. It was the only thing, right then, that was easy. Everything else, like trying to think about the mountains and Gabriel all at once, two things, that was hard.

One thing I knew. I never expected to feel like this on the day I heard I was to go to the Mountains of the Sangre de Cristo. For me such a day was going to be the biggest holiday, the best fiesta. Now this day was here. And there was only one thing to think about. That was Gabriel. Because next to my grandfather and father, next to my uncles

180

and my big brother Blasito, Gabriel was certainly the greatest man, for me, in the world. It was hard to think how anything could be good unless he was there, along with everybody else, to see how it was good. It was hard to think he wasn't going to be there, or anywhere that I knew about, how I couldn't yell "Gabriel" and he would come out from where he was—it was hard to think how this would be.

I kept tossing the rock. And I went back to take a look, around the edge of the house, at the mountains. They were there all right. I expected them to be. But everything else was so little like the way I expected, I just thought I'd have a look. They were there in the sun, the Mountains of the Sangre de Cristo, and they looked wonderful. And to think that in two days I would start, that I was going up into the mountains and up to the very top—that was hard to think about, too. And not only think. Also, even to look.

There was too much that was good mixed up with bad to know what to think. I turned around and let go with the rock. I hit the left-hand post of the gate. I had to find Gabriel. So I went into the house, running.

I found him going into the bedroom, from the parlor, waiting for me because I yelled his name when I got into the house.

"What are you going to do?" I asked him.

"I'm going into the bedroom to change my shoes. Why?"

"I mean about what I heard? How you had to go away?"

"There's nothing for me to do about it." He pointed to

181

a kind of dresser we keep in the parlor that has candles on it in glasses and a holy statue. "There's the letter."

It was leaning against one of the candles, a long letter. In one corner it said SELECTIVE SERVICE SYSTEM, with a lot of little words underneath. And in the middle, made with a typewriter, it said *Mr. Gabriel Chavez*, and underneath, also with a typewriter, our address.

"Mr. Gabriel Chavez," I read it out loud. "That's the right name. I guess it's no kind of mistake, hey?"

"No. Such a letter isn't often a mistake."

"Even if you got other things to do? The way you have to go with the flock this summer?"

"Well, I wasn't looking for this letter to come until next September or October. That's what the man in town told me, when I talked to him. But, here it is."

"Not until next September, October, that's what he told you?"

"Something must've happened, so it came now."

"I guess that's what it was," I said. "Something happened. I'm sorry."

"What's there to be sorry about? The army? It's nothing so much, Miguel. Our own father, he was in it before we were born. And Uncle Eli, during the last war. You remember how he talks about it. How good the food was. It's even better now. And the uniforms, they're better, too. I'll send you a picture, a special one for you, how I look all dressed up. You can show Juby and the others."

"Thanks," I said. "But that's not what I'm sorry about, how good the food is and the uniforms."

"No reason to be sorry, Miguel. Most of the kids from high school get drafted. What's so terrible?"

"Most? Not all?"

"Some don't. For one reason or another."

"Well, that's what it is, what I'm sorry about." Because for Gabriel there wasn't one reason or another. "Gabriel," I said, "do me a favor."

"Sure. Anything."

"Look, you can do what you want. And what I want to ask you is about this letter, to get rid of it. Don't go away. You can do many things, hard things. I've seen you. A letter can't be so hard, to get rid of it. So you can stay here on the place, with the rest of us."

"That's one thing I can't do, Miguel," he shook his head. "Get rid of a letter like this. But don't you worry about it." With his fist he made like he was punching me on the chin, only in a soft way, sliding across my chin, barely touching. "You just take it easy. I got to get some shoes on and get into town to see some kids. Take it easy."

And he left me. Standing there in front of the letter. And in front of the statue. Standing there, I knew what was the one reason for all this. I'd made a wish. Now I was given my wish. What I said to San Ysidro, he heard. This was not just my idea anymore. It was not something I decided in my own mind. It was real. My father said, "Yes."

183

I was going as I had made the wish to go. I was going because the letter had come. The letter was my fault. What was good and what was bad, both mixed together, all this was my fault.

It was I who had done this thing.

There was only one thing left that I must do.

CHAPTER 12

WHEN I got outside of the house to where I could be alone, the day was getting to the end and the sun was going down. It was the time of late in the afternoon when there would be Vespers if this was any kind of a holy day. And, in one kind of a way, for me it was.

It was like the other time at Vespers, too, the way the sky was, with gold and red, all rough together, and some pink.

I went way out into the field and stood there by myself

looking at the Mountains of the Sangre de Cristo. The mountains were lighter than any other part of what you could see, because on the mountains there was still some sun.

I stood for a while just looking at them, and then the time came for me to make my prayer. There was no reason to wait any longer. I knew now how to talk to San Ysidro so he heard me. That was sure. And I didn't have to make anything up. I knew what I had to say, and I knew how to say it.

So I clasped my hands together and closed my eyes tight, and I prayed.

"San Ysidro. Dear Sir. This is one of the Chavez family by the name Miguel. The one who spoke to you the other day about going up into the mountains. It was a hard wish for you to arrange, I know. And I want to thank you for taking care of it, except I didn't know you'd do it by a letter. I said fix it up whichever way you could, so that part is my fault. Only I didn't know you'd do it by a letter. I guess that's the only way you could do it. But the thing is this. If it's all right with you, I'd like to get my wish back. I don't want to be a lot of trouble for you, but the way things are, about going up into the Mountains of the Sangre de Cristo, I'd just as soon wait around for another four, five years, however long it takes, and then go when the regular time comes for me to go. So if you can just do me this one favor and forget I said anything or made any kind of a wish, and if you'd just take the letter

and get rid of it any way that you can, I'd thank you as hard as I can and say all the Hail Marys and other different kinds of prayers I can find. Only take away that letter right away, somehow, because it has to be now, and—that's about all. Amen."

There was a lot more I could have said, but there was no use taking up too much of his time, San Ysidro, because there can't be anyone busier than a saint. So I left it at that.

When I opened my eyes it was darker. There was no more light left on the Sangre de Cristo. But I didn't go from where I was standing until I said three times over, "Our Father Who Art In Heaven."

I thought about singing a hymn, too, but I wasn't sure of getting through one, all the words, without making a mistake. So I didn't.

By then it was real dark. And by the time I got back to the house all the lights were on.

I was scared to open the front door to look at the dresser in the parlor where the letter was.

When I did, it was no good. San Ysidro wasn't going to help anymore.

The letter was still there.

CHAPTER 13

THE next morning though, there wasn't any letter. Not on the dresser that stood in the parlor. Not in the house. By then it had disappeared altogether.

I was out at the woodpile when Gabriel found out. I was out there getting a load of wood for the stove to make breakfast, and I don't know why he should figure that it was me who had anything to do with what was missing. But he did. He came out of the house, putting on his shirt and stuffing it into his pants, looking for me.

"You," he yelled, "Miguel."

I looked up, but I didn't say anything.

"The letter on the dresser? The one from the draft board?"

I didn't say anything. I'd already counted up to six sticks of wood in my arm, because ten sticks make one load. Now I started to put them back, six, five, four.

"What happened to it?"

Why he should figure it was me? I started to walk away, sort of toward the river.

"Hey, you," he yelled after me. "You. Come back here!"

But I kept on walking, a little faster. And Gabriel, too, started to walk a little faster.

It was a good day to go fishing. I headed toward the river, running every third step. Then every second step. Then just running. When he saw this, Gabriel ran after me.

"Where do you think you're going?" Gabriel yelled to me.

Instead of any answer, I started to run my best. Gabriel, too. We headed down past the fence of the big corral. At the start, we stayed pretty even. When it comes to running, I'm a pretty good runner on account of the way I keep moving my legs up and down without getting tired, so I go pretty fast. But Gabriel is much better. Besides he's got longer legs.

We turned the corner at the end of the corral. We started up around the bend in the hill to where there's a path that goes down to the river. By then, it was not so even. I could see that in about thirty or forty more steps, all

190

Gabriel would have to do is to reach out and hold me by the neck.

When he caught up, that would be that. All I'd be able to do then would be to stand around and answer what he had to ask me.

So I stopped, in one step. And Gabriel stopped, too.

Once he asked me so that I had to answer, I couldn't say, "No." That would be too big a lie, too big a one, anyway, to stand for very long. So there was no use running. Instead I walked down to the river. Gabriel came down the hill after me. Down on the bank of the river, right near the water, I pointed out where was this rock. Gabriel lifted the rock, and he found the letter where I hid it.

"What's the big idea?" he asked me.

"Not so big," I said. "I just wanted to get rid of the letter so you wouldn't have to go way from here. That's all."

"That's all, hey?" He looked at the letter in his hand. Then he sat down, half kneeling, sitting on the back of one foot. He still kept looking at the letter like he was trying to read it without taking it out of the envelope. "Why is it, you don't want me to leave? Why not?"

"Because it's better when you're here, I think, everything's better." I went over and sat down the way he did. "Do you want to leave?"

"I don't know yet." Then he looked at me. "Anyway, I want to thank you for fixing me up with the draft board, and the United States Government, and the General Staff of the United States Army."

"It's nothing," I said. "Not for thanks, anyway. But how did you know it was me?"

"I sort of figured. Yesterday when we talked, you looked like you were fixing to do something."

"Oh," I said. "Well, you figured good. How about now, though, can't we put the letter back under the rock? And go home and have some breakfast and forget about it all?"

Gabriel laughed, not like there was a joke or anything, he just made the face for laughing and the noise.

"It'd be nice if it was that easy. But it's not the letter, Mike. That's not what is important. The letter don't mean anything. It tells me where to report, that's all."

He started to tear it up, the letter, to tear it up in little pieces. I watched him, and he started to throw the little pieces of the letter into the river.

"Getting rid of the letter," Gabriel kept tearing and tossing the papers into the river, "that won't change anything."

"No?" It was hard to believe. "Not a thing, nothing?"

"Look!" He ripped up the last pieces smaller and smaller. He threw them out into the ripples. He showed me his empty hands.

"And still you got to go?"

He nodded his head, yes. And for a while we just watched the papers sailing down the river. For such little bits of paper the ripples were big waves. And where the water curved around small rocks was like rapids. Two or three

192

pieces got caught on stones and branches. But they couldn't hold on long. The water shook them this way and that, until the papers let go and followed the rest. Then there was only the river going by making sparkles in the sun.

"Come on, Mike." Gabriel slapped me on the knee. "Thanks for trying, *hombre*, but we'd better get going now."

"Can't you wait, Gabriel? There must be some way," I asked him, "a good way to fix it so you don't have to leave here, the family and all. So you can stay and be a part of the way things happen here?"

"No, there's no way." Gabriel sat back on his heel again. "Besides, what's the difference? If it wasn't now, it would be after the summer. It's something you have to do, that's all, everybody."

"Some don't. That's what you said yesterday. Remember. For one reason or another, you said, some don't."

"Well, as far as that goes, Mike, you can hope a little if you want to. But there's only one chance in too, too many. So what's the use? Besides, it's no good to take it so hard, there's nothing so bad about the army." He stood up. "Once you get over wondering why you have to go at all, it's not so bad."

"If that part makes you wonder." I looked up and he took my arm to help me straight. "I know about that, why you have to go. That's something I have to tell you."

He stopped helping me, instead he came down to where I was.

"It's me," I explained to him. "I'm the only one who *does* know why you have to go."

"Well! You're the one I've been looking for, then," said Gabriel.

"It's my fault."

"You got in touch with some general you know?"

"Bigger than a general. San Ysidro. I made a wish. And that's why you have to go."

"A wish, *mi amigo*?" Gabriel looked at me in a puzzled way. "This is something I want to hear."

I told him about it, about everything. He listened to every word, without stopping me. And there was no noise or anything to get in the way. Just the river going by, soft. I got everything straight. So he understood everything. Even about the night before. How I tried to get the wish back, and I couldn't.

"That's why," I finished what I had to tell him, "it's because of me. My fault."

Gabriel didn't say anything. He picked up pebbles and jiggled them around in his hand, looking at the way they bounced.

"Isn't it?" I asked him.

"Well, it's a dangerous thing making the kind of wish you made, wishing so hard. That kind always comes true, one way or another. Sometimes in a way that surprises you."

194

"Then it is my fault?"

He looked up from the pebbles and studied the river, my big brother, then he said, "Yes. I guess it is, Miguel. Part of it is your fault."

"Well, that's why yesterday when I first heard about the letter, there in the parlor, when I was talking to you and you showed me the letter, I said I was sorry. Because I didn't know when I made my wish to San Ysidro that there would be anything like this. And if I did know, then all I want to say is—"

"Take it easy," said Gabriel.

"All right." I looked at the river along with him.

"It's only partly your fault. Part of it is mine too."

"How?"

"I made a wish, a real hard wish the same as you."

"No? To San Ysidro?" I was surprised. "To go into the army?"

"No, not exactly. Maybe San Ysidro knows about it, but no one else. Until now. I can tell you because it's something you'll understand."

"I'll try," I said.

"It's not about the mountains. It's not about anything that's here. You understand, Miguel, I like it here. I wouldn't want to live anywhere else."

"That much," I told him, "I understand."

"Yet for a long time too I've been looking at this river, the Rio Pueblo, and thinking. I've been thinking about all the places this river goes. Down to the Rio Grande and the way it goes through Texas, all the way down to the Gulf of Mexico. This water we're looking at, it's hard to think all the places it's going to, until at last it's out there way out in the ocean. This water, right here."

With his thumb he shot one of his pebbles, and we watched it splash.

"I've never seen an ocean," said Gabriel.

"I understand," I said. "Not around Los Cordovas. Only mountains and mesas and prairies."

"And so I thought how it would be to see an ocean once. Just for a while, to see an ocean and then to come back here and go on like always. To see all that water and the big waves, how an ocean looks. And the islands with water all around coming up white on the beaches, islands where the coconuts come from."

"To put on the cake," I nodded. "I understand about coconuts."

"It grows like footballs on trees. And on the same islands are girls that wear skirts made out of grass."

"What kind of grass, alfalfa?"

"A straw kind of grass."

"That must be interesting to look at. And cool."

"Well, that's been my wish for a long time, to go see an ocean, the Pacific, and the islands that are down there in the middle of it. And now, I've got my wish."

"But to be a soldier, wasn't that part of it?"

"No. That part was the surprise."

"I understand."

"I just kept wishing to go, that's all. I never said how, or in what way. So I'm going. If I don't like the way I'm going, that's my fault."

"Me too, Gabby. It's the same with me. That's what I told San Ysidro last night. It's my fault. When I asked him to arrange about the mountains, I told him any way that he could he should do it. That's why. It's not his fault, but mine."

"Yes," said Gabriel. "Both of us."

He flipped a pebble. And I found a pebble and flipped it, too.

"I understand now," I said, "how it should be done. When I talked to him, San Ysidro, I should've put in an 'only.' You know. Like he should fix it and all, *only* in a way that my brother Gabriel didn't have to go away for two years in the army. You, too. You should've put in an 'only.' "

"No," Gabriel shook his head. "That's no good. Where would you stop? You'd have ten dozen 'onlys.' "

"Why?"

"Well, you wouldn't want anything to happen to your father or mother. Or Leocadia or any of the girls and your brothers and your uncles and Grandfather and cousins. Or even to the sheep, or the house. Where would you stop? And how could you think of enough 'onlys' to cover everything? If you left out one, you could kill somebody that way."

"Then how can you make any wish at all?"

"If you ask me, you can't. It's risky. Unless you don't care what happens."

"I see." It sure didn't sound like a good way to live. "You mean there's no way you can wish for anything anymore?"

"Maybe little things. Everyday things. But to wish hard for something important? Then it looks like you got to be ready for the worst."

We sat watching the river go past. Both of us not talking because both of us were studying, I guess, what we just figured out. I felt around for a pebble. I couldn't find one the right size. Gabriel handed me one of his. We made two splashes in the river, right together.

"I never expected it like this," I said. "To find out this. How you can't go think what's good any more and then go wish for it."

"It's tough in a way but—" Whatever else he was going to say, he didn't; and I kept thinking about how it was going to be from now on with nothing to wish for. After a while Gabriel tapped me on the knee. "How about getting back? I could eat."

We went up the hill, both of us walking slow. Not like when we came down, when all I thought I had to do was show Gabriel where I hid the letter. Nothing was the same, somehow, the way it was when we came down. Not that anything you could see had changed. The sky was blue and the mountains far away, and there were clouds like before and the sun shining. But the way it felt was—heavy. Like everything was built where it stood, even the clouds, and was never going to move any more. Heavy, wherever you looked, and in place.

Gabriel went a little ahead of me. And then, because of his long legs, even walking slow he got pretty far ahead. I had a lot of things to think about, all the ones I couldn't wish for after this morning. When I looked up Gabriel was waiting for me at the top of the hill.

"Look, Mike," he said. "It's just something I thought of, you know. I could be wrong."

There was kind of a stone up there, kind of round. "What you thought don't look to be wrong." I kicked the stone and it rolled pretty good. "I can't see any mistakes you made when you figured it out."

We walked up to where the stone stopped and I kicked it. I got pretty good distance, only this time it went over on Gabriel's side a little.

"Still, it's only one man's opinion." We came up to the stone, and Gabriel shoved it back to my side with his toe. "After all, it's not like it was in the Constitution."

"Maybe not. But it's pretty clear," I said. "The way you can't use any 'onlys.' And the worst can happen. The way it looks is, no more wishes."

I lifted the stone this time, two or three inches off the ground. It went about ten, twelve feet.

"But look, Mike." Gabriel stopped me from walking. He kneeled down, sitting on his heel again, so we could look at each other. He took hold of my knee. "Why's it so much difference? Nothing's different. Tomorrow is the same as before. You're getting started tomorrow to go up there, with the others. You're doing a man's job this summer. A regular job. You're one man, along with the others."

"What?" I said.

"A man's job. So you got to forget what being a kid is like."

"I see."

"You can't go around making wishes, like Faustina, and expect some fairy godmother with a wand to come down and, *bueno*, make it all come true. For whatever you get, you got to give something." He pointed with his head to Taos. "Sure, Faustina can stand in front of Ilfeld's Department Store and she can wish her lungs out for a pair of shoes in the window. She doesn't see there's a price tag on the shoes with, maybe, the price $2.49. She just keeps on wishing so loud she stops traffic. But it doesn't do her any good, Mike, you know that. Nothing does any good. Until Mother goes in and talks business to someone behind the counter and pays two dollars and forty-nine cents. Then Faustina gets her wish. Only then. You have to give something to get it. That's how you got your wish. You gave something. And that's how I got mine. Now, do you see?"

"I think so."

"But that's one of the things you got to see," he held my knee tight, "when you get to be grown up, a man."

"Then," I said, "I see."

Gabriel let go of my leg. We walked up to where the stone was. I kicked it forward a little to Gabriel's side and he kicked it back.

"I see," I said. "The whole thing's like paying for what you get. Mr. Ilfeld is in business. And so is San Ysidro. It's like Uncle Eli says. Everything. Just dollars and cents."

Gabriel put his foot on the stone when I went to kick it. "Don't get me wrong." He looked down at me. "It's not only like that. Cut and dried like that. Business. It's only the way it happens with, well, everything. No matter what. Take a horse—you got to give him a day's feed to get a day's work."

"If you don't," I understood what he was saying, "he'll lay down and die on you."

"That's right. So it just isn't business, Miguel. It's a law. A universal, natural law. You only get when you give. It's a law like gravity."

"About that," I didn't know what he was talking about, "I'm sorry."

"Gravity? That's a law too. It pulls things together. Like, everything that goes up must come down. That's another universal, natural law. And everybody's got to obey it."

"Not saints."

"Sure, saints. Along with horses. Along with everything."

Gabriel took his foot off the stone, and I kicked it. We started for where it went.

"And if you're grown up," I asked him, "that's the way you got to think?"

"Why not?"

"No reason why not, except it ain't true, is it?" Gabriel was going to kick this time, but when he kept looking at me I took his chance instead. "I didn't know you had to stand that big a lie. Because he can go up without coming down, a saint can, can't he? And once he goes up, he can stay right up there. Saints sit around on clouds talking Latin and singing hymns without bothering about any laws. Or coming down. That's what's true, isn't it?"

Gabriel didn't answer me. He didn't do any kicking, either. He let me take the next couple of chances, and by that time we got back to the fence of the corral. "Isn't it true?" I asked him again. "They don't have to keep going up and down. A saint can go up and stay there and sit on a cloud all day long if he wants to. Can't he?"

"Not exactly." Gabriel kept feeling around in his ear for something. "It's one of those things you can't say is exactly true. Scientific."

"Then what happens?" I asked him. "When you grow up? You got to forget about everything you knew before? And think about everything different?"

"No." Gabriel's ear was giving him a lot of trouble. "It's not exactly that way either."

"But if they got to obey the law, saints, that's one thing. If not, that's different. It makes all the difference, don't it? About wishes and everything."

"I guess it does."

202

I kicked the stone again and followed it. "I sure thought when it comes to an important thing like this," I said to Gabriel, "someone would know for sure."

But Gabriel wasn't there. I'd left him behind. He was leaning against the fence.

"Mike, you're getting this all wrong," he shook his head. "You don't have to stop believing in everything you know. Sure, saints can stay up there on a cloud talking Latin. But when they come down here—" He stopped with a surprised look on his face. He snapped his fingers. "I think I got it! It's okay, Miguel. I got it!"

He came over to me with a big smile on his face, and he grabbed me by the neck and shook. My head wobbled. But not so hard, it felt good.

"You ought to be glad you got me for a brother." Gabriel laughed. "A smart son-of-a-gun like me."

"I am. Except now you're getting me dizzy."

"You dizzy? Me, that's what I am. I never even thought about these things before. But now it's clear. If you have to think about saints floating around up there singing hymns, that's okay. They don't have to obey any laws up there. As long as they stay up there. But once they come down, get mixed up with us, that's different."

"How?"

"It's just the same as if you went down to old Mexico, you'd have to obey the laws down there. Even though you're a United States citizen. Or if you went to France or Turkey, they got their own kinds of laws. And if you wanted to stay in their country, you'd have to go along with them, or get out."

"That's only right."

"It's the same here. We got gravity. And San Ysidro and the rest, when they come down they got to respect the law of gravity. They can't behave so that people go shooting off all over the place, like rockets on the Fourth of July."

"That's right, too."

"And if they give us a wish, they got to abide by the law, the law we have, and take something. Even if they don't want to. Because down here you can only get something if you give. Even if they wanted to, Mike, they couldn't give us a wish for nothing. Because things got to happen to us in only just the regular ways. And saints got to go along with that like everyone else. And that's why, when you get your wish, you can always be sure there's a surprise coming along."

"I see what you mean," I said. And I leaned against the fence to think about it.

If that was part of being grown up, to think out everything as smart as Gabriel, that part wasn't going to be easy. I could do the work all right. Like I told Pedro when he asked me at the shearing, the work wasn't too hard. But to be one smart son-of-a-gun the way Gabriel was?

I went over what he told me, in my head, to see if I could understand the way he did.

"Where are you?" Gabriel had kicked the stone twice and now he was looking back at me. "You coming?"

"Right away," I said. "I just want to figure a second."

He watched me, then he said, "I'll wait for you at the woodpile. We'll bring in the wood you came out for."

He picked up the stone we'd been kicking and threw it, in a big curve sharp against the sky, clean over the edge of the hill. It must've dropped into the river. I never could throw that far.

He went over to the woodpile and sat down looking at me.

I tried to think. About why there was no more wishes. It sure didn't make you feel good to know this. But that's the way it was going to be. If you were grown up, that's what you had to know. San Ysidro and the others, they couldn't do anything about it. They had to take something just the way you paid for shoes down at the department store.

Except?

I looked where Gabriel was. He was sitting on the woodpile, whistling the song about the girl with the red flower. With a stick he was drawing lines in the dirt, waiting for me.

Except, there was one big question. One we didn't figure out. I could understand about paying. But why couldn't you get your wish back if you had to pay too much? If you had to give so much you didn't want it anymore, why couldn't you get your wish back?

That's what they let you do down at Ilfeld's. If you de-cided it cost too much money, or for any reason, you could bring your shoes back. They had a sign there, on top of the mirror, Money Cheerfully Refunded. It was made out of gold words. Maybe that was a law too, a natural kind of a law, Money Cheerfully Refunded. Yet San Ysidro, when I asked him to keep Gabby out of the army and to forget my wish, nothing doing. Why? Why wasn't he just as cheerful as Mr. Ilfeld?

"Hey, you!" Gabriel banged the ground with the stick. "I'm getting hungry."

"One more second." I wanted to figure this one out for myself. There had to be some reason. And maybe I was smart enough to think what it was. Without asking Gabriel.

But I couldn't. There was no law he'd have to break, San Ysidro, to let you have your wish back. None that I could see. Or any other reason that I could see. Then why didn't he?

"I'm starving!" Gabriel stood up. "Come on!"

I started down along the fence. Gabriel had an armful of wood piled up when I got to him. It was no use, I never would know unless I asked him.

"Why don't they let you take your wish back, if you want?" I picked up some wood, too, because it would save me a trip later. "I mean, if you're not satisfied like with shoes, then San Ysidro why can't he be just as cheerful as Mr. Ilfeld?"

"I don't get it," said Gabriel.

206

"When I asked him to let the whole thing go and keep you out of the army, why wouldn't he?"

"Oh, that," said Gabriel. "That's very simple."

I knew it would be.

"The reason he can't is this." Gabriel took one of the sticks from the bunch in his arm and bending down, he started to point out on the ground. He didn't point out anything, just made marks in the dirt. "By now the whole thing is official. To get me out of the army, San Ysidro he'd have to get in touch with the draft board. And the draft board would have to get in touch with the General Staff. And they'd have to get in touch with the President. And the President, he couldn't do anything about me, just one guy who's drafted, not after it's official. The only thing he could do maybe is fix up the whole situation, and get in touch with the English and the Russians and the Chinese. And fix it so there's no trouble in Europe and Asia or in any of those places. So they didn't need an army. But for Heaven's sakes, all on account of me? It's too much. Even for San Ysidro."

"Why? Would he have to break a lot of universal, natural laws?"

"No. It's not that, Mike." Gabriel made three lines in the dirt. "It's because of all the things he'd have to fix up Too many things."

"What kind of things?"

"Well, things in general."

"Then San Ysidro, why don't he?"

"Why don't he?" Gabriel straightened up. "How should I know?"

I didn't mean to start a fight. All I told him was the truth. The way he said it himself. "Because you're one smart son-of-a-gun."

He started to talk, Gabriel, then he stopped. Instead he gave me a suspicious look, like I was sneaking up to hit him with a rock.

"Are you trying to kid me?" he asked.

"But all I want to know—" How could he think that? "All I want to know is why San Ysidro, he don't go out and fix up things in general?"

"Is that all?" Gabriel dropped on the woodpile the stick he held in his hand. "I guess you'd get a good laugh if I tried to answer that one?"

"What's to laugh? That's the most important answer, isn't it?" I was still bent down from watching the way he drew lines in the dirt. I looked up at Gabriel, and I couldn't understand why he should get suspicious at me. "What good are any of the first answers if you can't answer this, the last one?"

"What do you mean me, I can't? No one can."

"All right then, I'm just trying to understand." I tried to smile up to him so he wouldn't be suspicious. "Now I guess I understand. When you're grown up you only talk about laws and gravity and scientific. You don't have to bother about the important answer."

208

"If that's the way you think I talk, you ought to listen to yourself some time." Gabriel threw the load of wood in his arm back on the woodpile. It broke with a crash into separate sticks, sliding down. "The way you talk is like a three-year-old. Why the moon? Why? Why? Asking questions like Faustina. Why do sheep eat grass?"

I stood up. I got up from bending over to look at Gabriel straight. For him to talk like this, it wasn't right. First to say I was grown up, a man. Then to say I was three years old and asked questions like Faustina.

"At least Faustina," I looked straight at Gabriel, "when she wants to say nothing she don't use words you got to think about. She says babaloo."

"Then go talk to Faustina." Gabriel kicked a piece of wood that was in his way and began to leave. "Don't talk to me."

"All right." I watched him walk to the corner of the tool shed. "I thought you wanted me to understand. But if you want I shouldn't talk to you, then all right, I won't."

He was gone. I stood with the wood in my arms. I picked up a couple more pieces. Now that Gabriel didn't take any, I piled up a full load, ten pieces.

I wasn't like Faustina. The way she cries, from time to time, is one of the things around the house you get to expect. But here I was grown up, if that's what I was, my first day grown up without even breakfast yet, and I was in trouble. Gabriel was the greatest man in the world, next to some others, for me. And now he didn't want me to talk to him. Just because of one question, we couldn't talk to each other anymore.

No question was that important. I could let the answer go, if I knew this was going to happen. But now that I did ask, it would be good if I could find the answer myself. That would be the only way to fix it with Gabriel. Then maybe he'd see it wasn't such a dumb question, if I knew why it was that San Ysidro didn't go out and fix up things in general. If I knew the answer, then he'd see for sure I wasn't trying to kid him.

And then I knew. I was picking up the last piece of wood and then I knew. It was no harder than taking a deep breath to think about it. It just came into my head and then I knew.

And all that was left was to get Gabriel and tell him.

I ran as fast as I could, with that wood in my arms, to the corner of the tool shed to reach Gabriel before he got to the house. And there he was. He wasn't on the way to the house. He was walking in a hurry back to where I was.

"Mike," he said. "I was coming back after you. Did you ever see a bigger jackass than the one you're looking at right now?"

"No." What a surprise to see him! "No, I never did."

"You're right, I'm the biggest." When he laughs, Gabriel, it's like the last bell in the afternoon at school, the one to go home which rings clear and happy. "It's crazy to be

210

mad," he said. "You and me. Especially right now, with tomorrow, and us taking off."

"I'm glad," we breathed hard at each other, "I'm glad you think it's crazy. And I'm glad it's all right I should talk to you again."

"Please, Miguel," he shook his head, "if you'd only forget that."

"It's nothing," I told him. "Because when I talk to you now I don't have to ask that question any more."

"Which one?"

"You know, about San Ysidro."

"That one! Good. We'll forget that, too." He took a couple of sticks from my arm. "Here. I'll give you a hand with the wood."

"I don't have to forget it. I know the answer," I told him. "I know now why he can't go out and fix up things in general. He doesn't have the time."

"You may be right there." Gabriel took another stick of wood. He started for the house. "If we don't get going we'll be out of luck for breakfast."

He walked pretty fast but I kept up with him.

"That's what I think, I'm right," I said. "He don't have the time because we keep him too busy. With all our own wishes I mean. Like yours with the ocean. And me with the mountains. So where would he get the time to take care of things in general?"

"Could be." Gabriel opened the gate to let me through. "I sure could use a cup of coffee."

"And not only us two," I gave him another stick of wood. "Think of all the other wishes there were on San Ysidro Day. Our whole family, except Pedro, who everything he has is enough. Our father, his wish, I think it was about the alfalfa field across the river. And all the rest of us, our mother and sisters and uncles and cousins. And then, besides, everyone else from Los Cordovas. Everyone with their own private secret wish for San Ysidro to work on. It must keep him plenty busy."

Gabriel didn't walk so fast any more. "And your idea is, we're all so selfish making wishes, that's why things don't get better?"

"That's only part. It's not only us in Los Cordovas." Now that he was walking slower, if I took big steps we kept up pretty good together. "We're only a special job for San Ysidro. Because for us he's a patron. Besides us there's farmers everywhere he got to take care of."

Gabriel looked at me like he saw something interesting on my nose. "And the thing is, nobody's wishing for anything except what he wants for himself."

"Millions of farmers."

"After all. It isn't just plain selfish." Gabriel kept studying what he saw on my nose. "Lots of times everyone needs help."

"To fix up cows with colic, alfalfa fields, sheep with fever. It all means millions of wishes for San Ysidro. And all of them hard ones, Gabriel, as hard as the ones we made,

212

you and me. So where would he get the time, even to take care of the wishes that's his regular work?"

"Much less things in general." By now Gabriel was walking so slow up the path to the house, I had to take steps that were small even for me.

"And if San Ysidro don't have the time, then it's sure the same with the other saints. San Francisco and San Juan and Santo Domingo and the rest. I don't know them all but there can't be more than a couple of thousand or so—saints, that is. And when you add the angels and the cherubs, even though there must be flocks of cherubs, how many would you say all together—ten, twelve thousand?"

"Around ten, twelve thousand."

"By itself, maybe, that's a lot. But when you think how many people there are. Not only farmers. But every kind."

"They'd all be pretty much the same. Each one mostly looking out for himself."

"But what I mean is, every kind of people. In Taos. And in Espanola, too. And Sante Fe."

"Albuquerque." We come to the veranda, and Gabriel leaned with one hand against the post to think about it. "Carson City. Denver. Chicago."

"New York." I knew a lot of cities. "Washington. Paris."

"Paris is French."

"Can't you make a wish in French?"

"Sure." Gabriel thought about that. "And in Brazilian. And in Russian and Australian."

"All those people." I touched Gabriel's arm, so he would look down at me. "I didn't feel so good about what you said, how I talked like a three-year-old. Now I can see, you were right. For me to think about saints sitting around on clouds singing hymns. Pretty dumb, heh?"

"Why?"

"Why, because. Where'd they get any time to sit around? My goodness! When you think of those ten, twelve thousand saints and angels and cherubs trying to take care of so many people making wishes. Running here and there and all over, sliding around corners, bumping into each other. It must be worse than Saturday afternoon in front of the five-and-dime."

"The five-and-dime!" Gabriel laughed. "Think of them going there for mountains and islands and convertible coupes. They must get a lot of calls for those, convertibles. Yellow ones."

"It's right, isn't it?" I held him by the arm. "Isn't that why things in general, they can't be made better? No matter how much they must want to fix things up, we don't give them the chance."

Gabriel kept laughing and at the same time he shook his head.

"But it's got to be," I told him. "The answer. What can they do, San Ysidro and the others, the way we keep shooting wishes up at them like those guns, you know, for airplanes."

"Anti-aircraft."

"Those. A million anti-aircraft guns. Shooting up into the clouds, in the night when everyone says their prayers. So many wishes shooting up, secret ones, hard ones, and every wish different."

"Gabriel!" It was my mother inside the house. "Come on, you two. We're clearing the table."

"Just another second," I yelled. I kept my grip on Gabriel's arm. "Isn't that it, the answer?"

"I think it is," said Gabriel.

It was that simple. As simple as my father said "Yes" the day before when he told me about the mountains. But yesterday was because the letter came. This was something I had to do, and I did it. Myself. I found the answer. And because of that, Gabriel and I we were friends again. Now I could laugh, too. I had as good a laugh as Gabriel.

"If you don't get in here," it was my mother again, "it won't be so funny, Miguel."

"Here we come," I started in. "Right now."

Gabriel stopped me. "What're you going to do about it?"

"About what?"

"About the answer you found?"

"Is there something to do? Isn't just to get the answer enough?"

"It'd be even better if there was something to do about it." Piece by piece, Gabriel started to take the rest of the wood out of my arms.

"Why ask me what to do? It's not like I've been grown up for very long."

"Not long enough to get stale. That's why I'm asking."

Gabriel had all the wood now, and he waited for what I had to say. I didn't know what to say, except the simplest things.

"All we can do is to stop right now, to make wishes. Because anyway, like you say, it's dangerous. And if a lot of people stop, then things in general might get better. Because they'd have more time, the saints and the angels and the cherubs. To take care of, like what you said, what's in Europe, and the General Staff and the Chinese and the draft board."

From the top piece of wood there stuck out a splinter. Gabriel leaned against the post and chewed on this splinter, listening to me. "That's what you're not going to do, not to wish. Is there anything you *are* going to do?"

"What is there? Except." Then I knew. "One thing is, next year on San Ysidro Day I'm going to say a new kind of prayer."

"What do you mean new?"

"Like when we all get out there and it's the Blessing of the Fields, I'm going to pray like this. 'San Ysidro. Dear Sir. This is Miguel Chavez who took up so much of your time last year. Things went all right last year, and I have no complaints. Thank you for last year. But this year, I haven't got any wish. No wish at all. All I wish, San Ysidro, is for things to be the way you wish. Amen.' "

"Amen." Gabriel spit out the splinter he was chewing.

"That's a good prayer. But I don't know how new it is. Didn't I hear something like it before?"

"How could you? I just made it up."

"Yes I know, but—anyway, it's a good prayer, Miguel. Thanks for telling it to me. And thanks, too, I want to thank you for getting rid of that letter."

"Why? It didn't do any good."

"In a way it did. Otherwise, we'd never get the chance to talk like this. Because now—you remember when you asked down there, do I want to leave and I said I didn't know yet? Now I know. I want to leave."

"Why, what's happened?"

"Now I know why I have to go. Up till now, I could've been one of those pieces of paper getting pulled down stream, for all I knew why I had to go. Now it's different. I know. And while I'm gone, Mike, you learn everything about sheep. So when I do come back, you and me, we'll be the best two whooping *pastores* in all New Mexico."

"All right," I said. "I promise. Is there anything else you want I should do?"

"No, nothing else." But he scratched his ear. "Except maybe, just a little thing."

"Like what?"

"Well, when you get up there in the mountains, each one carves their name on a tree wherever we make camp. And near the first sheep camp, I started to carve one other name, but I never did finish. And if I wait three years or so to

217

finish it when I get back, it will never look so good. The last letters will never match the first because of the way the tree bulges out where you cut it. All I want you to do is to put in the last part of the name I started."

"All right," I said. "What's the name?"

"Carlotta."

"Juby's cow?"

"Cow? What kind of cow?"

"My friend Juby's cow, Carlotta."

"This is a girl I know in Taos, Carlotta."

We both laughed. What a mistake! To think of carving the name of a cow!

The screen door banged. It was our father.

"You two!" He was angry. "Jokes. While you mother's waiting in the kitchen."

"I'm sorry, Father," I started to explain.

"But that's it." Gabriel interrupted. He gave me a look as if I knew what he was thinking. He explained to my father. "It wasn't jokes. We were saying our prayers."

"What prayers?"

" 'Our Father.' " Gabriel turned to me. "Isn't that so, Miguel? It sounded like 'Our Father' didn't it?"

"What sounded like it?" asked my father.

"Thy will be done," said Gabriel. "On earth as it is in heaven."

"Amen," I said because that's what you have to say, and my father had to say it, too. "Amen."

"It's just the same, isn't it, Mike?" Gabriel asked me. "I thought I heard it before. It's the same as the prayer you made up."

"I don't think so," I shook my head. "Thy? I don't know about thy. And will? I just said wish. It doesn't sound the same at all."

"Now listen! I don't know what you two are up to." My father looked first at one then the other. "Whether it's joking or praying. Whatever it is, each one has its time. And now!" He pointed at the door.

It was time to eat.

CHAPTER 14

WE LEFT the next morning, both, the flock and Gabriel.

As always, the time for leaving came when it was not yet light. In this earliest part of the day, all of us outside packing the gear on the mules, it was like shadows working together. You had to look close to make sure who you were looking at. Everyone's face looked tired. There had been much work to get ready. And little sleep. No one went to bed in the regular way. Only naps, with your clothes on, on the couch in the living room or any empty bed there was around.

During the afternoon the day before, they brought the mules in. Pablo came from Eli's place and the other two, Herman and Rosalie, from Bonifacio's. It was necessary to shoe the mules as well as the horse, Blackie, because there were many long stretches on the trail that was nothing but rocks and stones, and without shoes the animals go lame. Blasito and Eli took care of shoeing them in the tool shed, where they built a fire. The fire was to heat the horse shoes so the iron could be shaped to the right size for each hoof, by hammering. Always before I used to watch how this was done. It is very interesting to see how Eli works as a blacksmith and especially how much he sweats, but now only Pedro watched by himself.

I helped Uncle Bonifacio get down the big tent from where it stayed all year in the loft above the shearing shed. We spread it out on the ground in the barnyard to see if it was in good shape. And it wasn't. There were tears and holes, and the ropes had many knots and were frayed at the end like brushes.

"Every year the same thing," Uncle Bonifacio shook his head. "Always the last minute before we fix up the outfit. This year will be different. You and me, Miguel, we'll fix up everything before we put it away, you and me, when we come down this year."

"I'm sorry," I told my Uncle Bonifacio. "I can't think about coming down, yet. Only about going up."

Uncle Bonifacio smiled to say, all right. But the truth is I didn't do much thinking about going up. It was too close, now. And too much to do. While he and I fixed new ropes into the different parts of the tent, my mother and Leocadia helped to patch it. They mended up the tears and sewed new pieces of canvas over the holes, using big needles and heavy thread, working on their knees where the tent was spread out in the barnyard.

On the porch, my father arranged all the things we were taking along to eat. There was food enough, big and little boxes, cans and sacks, to set up a grocery store. But even so, my father went into town during the afternoon and came back with more. We could eat for years the way it looked, not months. There were sacks of beans and great cans of flour. In the flour was packed the eggs, because it was soft and tight and the eggs would not break. There was bacon and ham and salt meat, and many cans, some with vegetables and others with fruit for dessert, and also others with jams and jellies, including grape which is the best kind of jelly. There was much tobacco for the men, and big bags of salt, most of which was for the sheep. The salt for the sheep is coarse and looks like rock candy, which is what the sheep must think it is, the way they eat it. There was real candy, too, for us, and a burlap bag of coffee, and a box filled with milk in cans, and so many other things that, like every year, I never believed the mules would carry so much.

But they do. Most of the food is packed in canvas bags, and the mules carry them all easy. From the outside these bags don't look so big. But when you start putting stuff inside, the bags hold much more than you expect, like they were made out of rubber instead of canvas. The rest of the food and the pots and pans are put into special pack boxes. These, too, had to be repaired, and this work was done by Gabriel, who worked with a saw and hammer and other tools out in back of the house.

The boxes are like cupboards, made with the backs curving in so that the box can lay against the belly of a mule. Once they are hung on the pack saddle, you don't even have to take the box off the mule to use it. All you do is to lift up the front which is made like a door with hinges on top, and inside are shelves where everything is arranged like my mother's closet above the stove in the kitchen. It makes everything easy to use, especially on the trail when you stop to make dinner in the middle of the day. You don't have to untie the whole pack in order to get the things you need for cooking.

Gabriel did not finish with the boxes until, almost, it was getting dark. And the work of stowing things away went on all night long, the food and the bedding and ammunition for the two guns and all the rest, even medicine and a box of books which were mostly for my father and Bonifacio, who are the two you'll find reading books if there are any books around being read.

Outside, the work was done by the light of lanterns. There were lanterns moving around in the barnyard and out in back of the house, as well as on the road where the mules were. The lanterns here and there looked like *luminarias*, as if this were a holiday. Usually it is like a holiday the night before the men set out for the Mountains of the Sangre de Cristo. But not this time. On account of, in the morning, Gabriel was leaving for so long.

Because of this no one talked so much or went around laughing the way they usually did on this night. Of everyone, Gabriel himself was the most cheerful. So much, my mother said, "From the looks of you, Gabby, it was like you were glad to leave us."

"Sure," Gabriel laughed. "Here's where I start to eat some real good cooking."

My mother laughed as well, but not too hard.

And once, when I just came into the house, I heard Tomasita finish a long speech. She and Gabriel were by the washtub.

"You and Alfredo and Dick Montoya. It's a shame the way you're all going," said Tomasita. "Those politicians, I'd like to soak their heads."

"The first one I meet," said Gabriel. "I'll give him a towel and send him around."

"They're the ones who make all the trouble."

"Not for me." Gabriel shook his head. "I don't need anyone to make my trouble. I do all right on my own."

He saw me, and he winked. I winked back. I guess he and I felt better than anyone else in the house.

Along about the middle of the night, I got very tired from all the folding and lifting and putting away. My father told me to go sleep. The big chair in the parlor was empty, so I slept there. No sooner did I get settled than my Uncle Eli shook me. It felt only like seconds, but he told me that already it was getting close to be morning.

"Make a bundle," he said, "and bring it out on the porch. All your clothes and what you'll need."

"I know how."

It was hard to believe the night was getting finished. I made the same bundle I always did, only this time I put in the Indian stone because, I figured, you never know when you might need such a stone. I brought the bundle to the porch, which was now almost empty.

"You got everything in here?" Eli asked me when he took the bundle.

"My heavy mackinaw, and three pairs long drawers, and two sweaters, and the hat which comes down over my ears," and all the rest of the things I told him.

"*Bueno*," he said. "You know how to make a bundle good."

"Why not?" I answered him. "After so much practice."

He stuffed the bundle in the canvas duffel bag and took it out to where the mules were tied, to the white fence in front of the house. Except for Grandpa, who was having coffee in the kitchen, everyone was already out there working like shadows in the last hour of the night. Gabriel was there, too, all dressed up ready to leave, in a jacket that had only two buttons and a shirt with a tie on it. He looked already a little like a stranger helping Bonifacio tie up the mule Pablo.

To load a mule takes much practice. First, on top of blankets, goes a pack saddle, which is nothing but a pair of wooden pieces, crossed, that are strapped onto the mule like a regular saddle. Then all the bags are hung onto these crosspieces. Over everything you throw a poncho or a piece of tarpaulin. And the whole thing is tied down with a diamond hitch, which is a way of tying a rope—this way and that way and around and over—that takes a long time to learn. I've watched how it is done many times, but it's still a puzzle to me the way you make all the different knots. It's one of the things I must learn soon, because a diamond hitch holds a pack on a mule like the pack was bolted down.

By this time, Blasito, on the horse Blackie and with the dog Cyclone, had worked the flock of sheep up from the river where they had their last drink. It was the only water they would have for all day, which is not too hard on the sheep because they can go many days, if necessary, without water. They spread out in the fields across the road, the flock, all the ewes and their lambs, almost eighteen hundred animals.

By now, too, it was getting gray with light.

I saw my father and Gabriel standing by the fence talking very serious for a long time. Then my father took Gabriel in his arms and kissed him, first on one cheek then on the other. And I knew it was now time to say goodbye.

Gabriel came to where I was standing. He gave me his jackknife.

"So you can do me my favor," he said. "And finish the T-T-A."

"For such a little favor, I don't need such a good knife, with a corkscrew and can opener both."

"I'll get another knife from the army."

"All right, then," I said. "Thanks."

"Well, now," said Gabriel, "I guess we should wish each other good luck."

"How?"

"Just by saying it." He put out his hand to shake. "Good luck, *mi amigo*, good luck to you."

"Good luck, Gabriel." We shook hands, and that was the way we said goodbye.

I went and shook hands with everybody, except my mother, who I kissed. She told me to be good, and I promised. My grandfather told me to take good care of the sheep, and I promised. Leocadia told me to keep my feet from getting wet, and I said I'd try. Tomasita told me not to go too far away from the others, and I said only if I had to. Blasito told me to bring back a mountain lion, and I said I'd try. Faustina told me, "Pocoloco," which didn't mean anything like always, so I said, "GalgoGalgaleno, Faustina." And then there was Pedro.

He gave me his hand to shake.

"Goodbye," he said, "whatever you name is."

"That part is settled," I told him.

"What is it? Twister, Miguel, Babaloo?"

"Chavez."

He laughed, surprised, "Me, too."

We shook hands, and my goodbyes were finished.

Already Eli was in the saddle on Blackie, leading out the mules, each one tied to the one before. Eli was to be the camp tender, he was to cook the meals and take care of that part. Bonifacio, my father, and me, as well as Cyclone, were to drive the sheep. Bonifacio was already on the far side of the flock starting the sheep slowly to move. My father and I walked across the road. I heard the soft noise of galloping behind me and looked around. It was the orphan, Jimmy.

I looked at my father. "All right?"

"Well, now, Miguel, all the time the orphan is left," he started to tell me. But he finished. "All right."

So Jimmy followed me.

Before we reached the flock I heard the noise of the truck starting up back at the house. I stopped to look and saw Gabriel give my mother one last hug. Then he got into the truck beside Blasito, who was driving him into town. The truck started down the road in the direction opposite from the one we went. Going fast, it sent up a little feather of dust as it ran away from us. The flock went slow, but the dust it made was a big cloud rising up into the sky, which had become blue and bright because it was morning.

I turned back from looking at the truck and walked into the dust the sheep were sending up. Many times I had watched this sight from the house. Now I was helping to

228

make this cloud myself, and Jimmy as well, behind me.

Beneath our feet the earth was dry with the coming of summer. We were many feet. Four times eighteen hundred for the sheep. Four times four for the mules and the horse. Four times two for the men, which makes eight feet together. Four more for Cyclone, and four feet for Jimmy. Under so many feet the dirt broke apart and rose up like heavy smoke in the air. I walked right behind the sheep and swung my jacket, shouting like the rest of the men. We had to keep them moving, the sheep, to get them up off the flat before the hot time of the day began. From where I walked, in the middle of the drive, there was nothing to see. The mountains were nowhere. The other men, as well as Eli and the pack train, only shadows in the dust rolling up. I remembered how we looked. A brown cloud moving south, moving slow across the prairie, getting ready to start up and climb to where the other clouds were, round and white, 'way up there on the top. That was how we looked, the sheep and the men of the Chavez family, moving out to summer pasture.

The cloud that was us sailed slow past the town of Ranchos. I knew this was so because to the left and the right, in the dust, there was no more sagebrush or other bushes. It was all cut flat, and this was a place called the airport, right next to Ranchos. There were no buildings here, just a long flat stretch in the middle of the brush so that any airplane that had to land around here would have a place to land. Though not many airplanes did. Soon

229

the bushes came back and the ground was rough again, which showed that we were past the airport, and not very far beyond we came to the black-top highway that goes south to Espanola and Sante Fe. The cloud that was sent up by all the hundreds of feet that we were crossed over the highway, and now every time that we took a step it was just a little higher, not much, but a little higher than the step before.

I drove the sheep, going back and forth with my jacket, shouting, hurrying them along with the other men. It did not bother me that I could not see outside the cloud that we were raising. This was still the land of my childhood. I knew what was here because I had been to these places many times. To the east we passed the village of Talpa sitting there across the Arroyo Miranda. And then we passed the place where there is hot water coming out of the ground, called the Springs of Ponce de Leon, and where is a man who has built a pool there in order to charge, I think, fifty cents for anyone who wants to come swim in hot water.

To the west was the Arroyo del Alamo, a rocky, washed out place in the sun this time of the year, but a full river in the spring, black and white, rushing over the rocks. Though the sheep were spread out far to the left and the right, farther than I could see in the dust, we followed along the way of a trail that has always been here, called the Kiowa Trail. It is called after some Indian, I guess, but who he was, I don't know.

The cloud that was us turned a little to the east. It started up over one of the shoulders of Picuris Peak. I remained in the middle of the cloud. Each step now was surely up, with rocks to climb and cactus to go around. Keeping up, keeping after the sheep to get them to move quickly, getting after the lazy ones and bunching them up with the rest, it was not easy in all that dust; and the day, too, had now grown heavy with the heat.

I was glad to hear my Uncle Bonifacio yell. The sheep came slowly to a stop. It was time for them to rest through the hours that the sun was high and shining straight down. The flock broke up, a few here and there, in the little shade of the rocks and high bushes and the stubby pine trees. There was cool water for us to drink out of the canvas bags that hung on the mules, and sandwiches that we brought for our lunch. When they finished to eat, the men lay down where they found shade and slept with hats over their eyes. It was the time of siesta. I sat and looked back over the way I had come.

I could not see our house from the small height we had reached. But I knew where it was by one of the buttes that stood out of the mesa which is behind our farm. Between that place and the place where I now sat was where I grew up. I looked down now where my life had been for all the twelve years that I lived. Then I yawned, and I, too, fell asleep.

It was the beginning of the afternoon when we started again, and there were more shadows. We went over the shoulder of Picuris Peak and dropped down a little, so that the wide valley of the Rio Grande behind us was hidden. But not for long. We went up a slope called U. S. Hill, and the valley returned, looking now even wider, as we drove the sheep up.

Already we came to a part where I had never been before, a new part which I had never known. It did not look very different from what we left behind, all rocks and little bushes, juniper and chaparral as well as mesquite, and here and there a twisted tree of pine no higher than a big bush. The same dust. And again the hurry to keep the sheep moving. On top of U. S. Hill there would be the Ranger who was to count the sheep and see that we were bringing no more than we were permitted. The hour to meet him was fixed. So we hurried.

We moved quickly up U. S. Hill, a big cloud of dust with me in the middle. There was one problem. Where did they begin, the Mountains of the Sangre de Cristo? Somewhere the hills ended and the mountains started. It would be good if there was a sign saying, Now. But I never heard of such a sign, and there wasn't any. So what if, already, the mountains had begun?

There was shouts up ahead once more. We had come to the top, to the rocky crest of the hill, and just on the other side was Mr. Young, the Ranger, who had come to count the sheep. To count so many sheep is not easy unless there is a place to make them go in a single line so they pass you one at a time, and this way you can count them. There was such a place here. Coming down from the crest on the other side was a little narrow wash with steep sides. It led to a gate, which was part of a fence that stretched as far as you could see to the north and the south. Mr. Young stood at the open gate with my father, ready to count, and it was up to the rest of us to drive the flock through.

On the trail, in a strange place, sheep are afraid of everything. It was hard to get them started through the gate. The first sheep refused. They turned off to the north and the whole flock started to circle around on itself. It made twice as much dust as before, the frightened sheep running around, then stopping and going the other way, each one of them bumping the other, and all of them bawling at once, together. Like the whole eighteen hundred was in a choir, each one singing something different, only it wasn't singing, just yelling. One big mess.

Eli got them started finally. He shoved one of the sheep wearing a bell half through the gate, and after it stood there for a moment the ewe went the rest of the way through on her own. Once that happened, everything changed. You'd think on the other side of that gate, the circus had come to town. Every sheep in the flock wanted to be the next one through. They followed the leader with such a rush, the big job was to keep the sheep away from the gate so none of them would get hurt, all pressing in at once. The dust and the mess was as bad as before. Bonifacio, Eli, and I tied handkerchiefs around our faces so that we could get air to breathe without dirt.

The sheep went past my father and the Ranger with big jumps, like they were going over the gate instead of through it. It went fast. But Mr. Young didn't lose count. He had a special kind of a counting watch, with a lever that he pressed down as each sheep passed. So that he didn't have to keep the numbers in his head, he only just had to keep pressing as each sheep jumped by. With the ewes and the lambs shooting through, with Mr. Young clicking his watch, it didn't take too long, only a little longer than a half hour to get all the sheep counted.

It was long enough for me, working there in that narrow gully with all the dust and so hot. I was glad to see only a few sheep left and be able to get up to the gate myself.

When Mr. Young saw me he turned to my father. "Another Chavez?"

My father nodded his head. "Miguel."

"How you doing?" Mr. Young asked me.

There wasn't time for too big an answer so I just said, "Good."

He clicked his watch a couple of more times for the sheep going through. "First time you've been up here, in the Sangre de Cristo?" he asked me.

"Yes." I watched him work the watch. "Where do they begin, the mountains?"

"Begin?" He clicked some more. "Well, you might as well say they begin right around here."

234

With his other hand he waved behind him. I went through the gate ahead of the last bunch of sheep. I walked to where he pointed, to a bush all brown with the dirt that was flying. I walked around the bush, out of the brown air in which I had walked all day. I stopped. Mr. Young was right.

There they were.

I stood. I pulled down the handkerchief from around my face. In order to breathe better. But I don't remember breathing. I stood, that's all. Because there they were.

It was green. What was brown, what was gray, what was dry and old and burned up and dead, that was behind. Here was green. Folded together, and bunched up, rolling higher and higher, green. Right in front the green dropped away, it was a little valley that was a meadow with a creek curving through. Then it started—the green climbed, in round steps going up, pushing out here, then starting from behind and going up again, shelves of green, one on top of the other. The green went up and it went wide, far to the north where there was a white peak and far to the south where was another, a mountain white with snow in the sun. And all the rest green.

There was no more Miguel. Only a pair of eyes to look at the green, the great trees of pine and oak. Two eyes, and one nose to pull, like a lamb nursing, at how clean it was and sharp, to smell the chill that was here and the faraway, soft taste of the pine and the spruce. I stood there, no longer me, only a pair of eyes and a nose and two feet that had taken their first step into the Mountains of the Sangre de Cristo.

This was it.

This was the minute that divided everything. All the time before from what was here. Until this minute, everything important was ahead, what was coming, to wait for. From this minute, it was different. The most important thing was happening right now. To hope and to be afraid, to plan, that time was ended. There was nothing to do except in this minute, and that was to look and to breathe and to stand here, where I was.

This was it, the minute. And from then on, each minute was the same.

There is a time in our house, on New Year's, when everyone comes to watch the old alarm clock we have on the icebox in the kitchen. The house is crowded with all our family and many cousins and friends, and even Faustina and Pedro are allowed to stay up so that they, too, can look at the clock. Until the time comes, no one looks too much. But when the big hand gets up on the left side, getting near to the little hand which stands straight up, everyone crowds into the kitchen. It is so crowded, there is hardly room to sit down, and everyone stares over the shoulder of the other. At the clock.

Like something absolutely wonderful was going to come out of our old alarm clock, the way a fake bird used to come out of the clock of Mr. Hoffman, the saddlemaker in town, before it got broke and stopped running.

When the big hand gets near to the top, some one says, "Only four minutes left."

Then maybe a few people say, "Only three minutes."

Then all say, "Two minutes."

"One minute."

Then when both hands stand straight up, one covering the other, then that is the minute, the Big Minute, and from looking so hard, everyone busts out being as happy as they can, shouting "Happy New Year" and seeing how many people they can hug and kiss and punch and shake hands with while it still remains the Big Minute.

The truth is, the Big Minute would have to last a lot longer than it does for everyone to get around to everybody else. So by the time the rush for punching and kissing is over it's already maybe five minutes or so after the New Year. And that's about the end of it, as far as everybody busting out all at once goes. Faustina and Pedro get sent off to bed. And a little later, the way it used to be, me. And for the rest it becomes a regular party again, with only one or two or so kissing and punching, as the case may be.

But the way it was now, on the other side of the crest of U. S. Hill, with me looking and breathing and standing, it was like the two hands got up there to the top and stayed right there. Like they weren't going to move anymore. Like the Big Minute was now, and the next was the Big Minute, too, and the next and the next. Each one was the Big Minute, and never one minute to, or one minute after.

This was it.

It took us five days to get up to the place where we had our first regular sheep camp. Each minute was filled with what there was to look at and to breathe in and to feel. Not all were happy, or exciting or like that. There were all kinds of different minutes, filled with something that hurt, even, or something sad, or with being tired. But each one was important alone and by itself. None of them were only part of something that was before or followed after.

These are some minutes of the way we went up into the Mountains of the Sangre de Cristo.

It was the middle of the first night and there was a small thin moon. Our camp was across the valley from U. S. Hill on the side of Gallegos Peak. We slept outdoors under blankets and ponchos or in sleeping bags. I woke up looking at the fire, dark red coals growing black. I looked up at the stars, many stars, through the piñon tree. I looked around to the sheep; they were dark on the ground all around. But there were sheep who stood straight and still like on guard. Somewhere in the camp, Cyclone coughed in his sleep. It was warm under the blankets though my face was cold. I closed my eyes.

It was morning and we came to Quien Sabe Creek. Never before had I seen a river coming straight down,

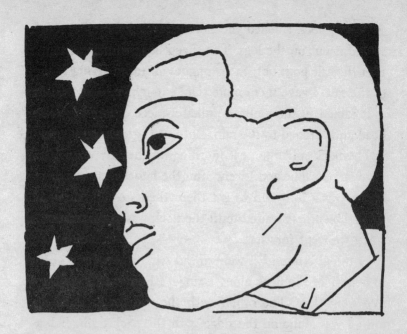

waterfalls all the way upstream until hidden by the trees. The flock stopped, not wanting to go across. I watched the water come jumping down, all bubbles, whipping and bouncing down. Bonifacio rushed the lead sheep across the creek, using a fallen tree for a bridge. The flock followed. I, too.

Going up the trail near Cerro Vista Mountain, I saw the name of my grandfather carved on a tree. The bark was puffed out and cracked, but the name was there to read. *G. Chavez. July 1st. 1901.*

That night we made camp on the other side of La Cueva Peak, and I laid out the salt for the sheep. There were logs hollowed out, which had been used many years to put the

239

salt. The flock smelled the salt and couldn't wait until I spread it out on the logs. The sheep licked my hand while I let the salt pour out, their tongues all rough trying to get to the salt. I gave them more than enough.

It rained in the night. I pulled a piece of tarp over my head and listened to the rain. But not for long.

The flock split the next morning on the way up Carpio Canyon. Cyclone and I went after the bunch that got away. There was a long run to get them then we headed them back. The others waited until the flock was together again. Then we went forward.

In the afternoon Eli went ahead with Blackie the horse to help herd the flock along a ridge. I led the three mules. We went slow. The others with the flock got far ahead, until I was alone on the ridge with the pack train. Below us were some of the lower peaks of the Mountains of the Sangre de Cristo. I stood and I looked down on them.

It was cold after supper. Before I went to sleep I put on my long drawers. It was the first time this ever happened in July.

When Eli and I were breaking camp the next morning, the sun came up red. I saw an eagle. This great bird can be bad for the lambs. But it went away.

Going up the trail above Serpent Lake, I stopped to watch the lambs be happy. It is easy for them. They stand on their hind legs and, without moving a muscle, they can jump high up and down. As if on the end of a rubber band. They like to jump over each other too. Watching

them, I stood among a bunch of trees, high fir trees and spruce and aspens, up to my ankles in soft needles. The air smelt cold and sharp and like there was fresh paint somewhere around. I couldn't jump like the lambs. But then, I didn't have to.

We had dinner at noon under small, twisted spruce trees at the edge of the timber line. Looking up from where we ate, there were no more trees. It's like we were coming out on the top of everywhere.

We passed over the crest of Jicarita Peak. This is the highest that we go, more than thirteen thousand feet above sea level. On the north side of the peak there are snow fields, many acres of snow. I walked in the snow and made snowballs on this day of July the fifth. I carried the snowballs in my coat and picked off any sheep that strayed away from the flock, not failing to hit one that I aimed at. The sheep didn't mind being hit with snowballs. Snowballs are softer, after all, than stones.

It rained in the afternoon, and there was fog when we were still on the high ridges of the Jicarita. There was nothing far as could be seen except rocks and boulders, no trees and not a blade of grass. It is lonely way up there above the timber line. I slipped in the rain and hit my knee on the point of a boulder. There was much pain in the bone of my knee. But this is no place for some one who cannot stand to be hurt. I rode behind Eli on Blackie. There was much jolting, and it was almost easier to walk.

We made a cold camp on the Jicarita because it got dark

so quick on account of the rain, and because of my knee. There was no wood for any fire. The only place to be warm was under the blankets. I thought of Pedro and Faustina. Then of my mother. After a while, about Tomasita and Leocadia and Blasito and Gabriel. I thought a long time about Gabriel and where he must be before I went to sleep.

I felt better the next morning. And it was easier to walk because the way was down. Soon we were back among the pine and fir trees, again, and the aspens.

I saw a tree with the name of my father. *Blas Chavez. June 1919.*

We made camp early in the afternoon in a meadow on the side of the Santa Barbara river. We wanted to give the sheep a chance to graze. Also to heat water to soak my knee. The sun came out and it was warm. After a while I found a wide pool in the river with a waterfall coming down, and we all went in for a swim. We found a place where the water came down over a long smooth rock into the pool, and we went sliding down like boys. My father, as well.

After supper around the fire that night we sang songs. I sang Gabriel's song about the girl with the red flower. For the first time I remembered all the words.

When I got up at dawn my knee felt good again. I helped to take the hobbles off the mules and Blackie, and to help pack the mules. I was almost able to tie the diamond hitch, but I missed on the last two twists of the rope.

We went up the Santa Barbara River, until we came to the Middle Fork where stands an empty cabin that is used by the Forest Ranger. This meant we were climbing close to the end of the drive.

I climbed up the hill after my father and the others and then through a high stand of pine trees. When I came out of the woods my father was standing alone before a wide pasture. The grass was high and there was a rushing brook with many pools. Good food for the sheep, and water. My father told me to throw away my stick. The drive was over. On the edge of this pasture was our first regular sheep camp.

I helped to set up camp, to bring water, to fix the iron stove, to chop wood, to put up the tent. My father said I had done enough. I had time to look around.

Across the meadow the land fell away, a great cliff looking down to the mountains and the country below. Here were trees with many names. I found the name that Gabriel was carving. It stood on the tree, *Carlo*. I turned to look at the world below.

In this place many men named Chavez had come. Those I could not remember, and then my grandfather as well. And my father, Blas and my uncles, Eli and Bonifacio. And my brothers, Blasito and Gabriel. And now, watching the shining world as I knew it would look when I came to this place, I stood, Miguel.

I took out my jackknife. There was a good tree where I could carve my name. But for that I had many weeks, and there were to be trees everywhere all summer long. First I would do the favor for Gabriel. To carve Miguel Chavez on a tree way up there on the top of the Sangre de Cristo is not so easy, because the name has in it many curved lines. It was easier to do the favor for Gabriel first and carve T-T-A, all straight lines, for a start.

ABOUT THE AUTHOR

Joseph Krumgold was the first writer to receive the Newbery Medal twice. He was awarded the medal, which is given for the most distinguished contribution to literature for children, in 1954 for ...AND NOW MIGUEL and again in 1960 for ONION JOHN.

Mr. Krumgold began his writing career in Hollywood. For more than twelve years he wrote and produced screenplays for several major studios. He then worked away from Hollywood on documentary films in which the story was given as much emphasis as the fact. These films earned the author first prizes at the Venice, Prague, and Edinburgh Film Festivals, a nomination for the Academy Award, and wide approval both in the United States and abroad.

Mr. Krumgold grew up near New York City, although he traveled extensively and lived in a variety of places, including California, Paris, and Rome. From 1947 to 1951 he spent most of his time in Israel, where he made movies throughout the conflicts that marked the founding of the Israeli nation.

ABOUT THE ARTIST

Jean Charlot was born in Paris of a Mexican mother and Russian-French father. In his early twenties he went to Mexico and he has been identified with the modern movement in Mexican art. There he helped revive interest in the lost art of wood carving, painted frescoes in various institutions, and illustrated books.

Later an archeological expedition took him to Yucatan to do studies of the bas-reliefs in the Temple of Warriors and then to Washington to work on two books that dealt with the Yucatan findings. He lectured at the Art Students League in New York, at the University of Georgia, at Columbia University, the University of Hawaii, and many other universities across the United States.

Although known chiefly as a muralist, Mr. Charlot was also a painter. His works are widely exhibited and hang in the Museum of Modern Art and the Metropolitan Museum of Art in New York.